FIVE STONES

Alaa's Quest

JAMIE LEE CARRIE

Library of Congress cataloging-in-publication data has been applied for.

FIVE STONES: Alaa's Quest.

COVER ART *Laila and Sheba* – J.L.Carrie

ISBN: 979-8-9918618-2-3 (PAPERBACK)
ISBN: 979-8-9918618-3-0 (KINDLE)
ISBN: 979-8-9926590-3-0 (HARDBACK)
ISBN: 979-8-9926590-0-9 (EPUB)

I am an AMERICAN author. I speak and write in the dialogue that is prevalent in the USA, specifically, in the southern states. If you are not familiar with this dialect, I do apologize. It is not considered proper KING'S ENGLISH, but it is proper spelling and grammar for my country of origin. Some phrases may have to be googled for better understanding. I hope it does not hinder your ability to read, understand, and enjoy.

For my children,

James, Caleb, Joel, Nathan, Landen, Tristin, &
Anisette. I love you.

~And, for Alaa.

A special dedication to all of the romantics, who still
believe that love and magic are intertwined.

PROLOGUE

EGYPT, 1801

There was a storm raging, unlike any Cairo had seen before.

She lay on her bed, exhausted. Sweat covered her face and glistened under the glow of candlelight. It had been four days. The only words uttered since the last nightfall were whispered pleas to God to lessen her burden and allow the child to come.

True to her nature, Laila's voice never rose above a timid tone, no matter how excruciating the pain. The gray color of her skin, sunken eyes, and pale lips told the midwife everything she needed to know— the battle was being lost.

The future contentment of the people depended on the highly anticipated birth. He needed to be alive and healthy, even if at the expense of his mother.

Another wave hit, contorting her face and forcing her upright.

They were running out of time, and she was out of energy to fight for either of them.

"Highness, please, do not give up!"

Hala's request came out sounding more like an

order than a plea. She felt immediate remorse as her own words echoed back to her in the little room.

They had been friends since they were small children, and the relationship they shared was more like that of sisters. The caste discrepancy never affected the love and loyalty between them. She had always been happy to serve her, and becoming her maidservant allowed them to remain together always.

She wiped a cool rag across Laila's forehead and gently pushed stray hair from her face. Cooing words of encouragement, she grabbed her hand and held it tightly as the next wave came. The pains were back-to-back, allowing no time for recuperation. Tears of empathy and grief streamed down Hala's face; she felt so helpless. For the first time in their lives, she couldn't help her. No matter how hard she tried to hide her emotions, she simply could not.

The midwife, haggard from the whole experience thus far, impatient, and obviously suffering from the pressure of it all, spoke harshly.

"Highness, with the next contraction, I will need you to lean forward, hold your breath, and *PUSH!* If you do not, the baby will surely die. You have a duty; you mustn't fail!"

As was customary, when it was announced that the time had come, family, friends, and officials gathered inside the palace walls to celebrate and wait. As time wore on and complications became apparent, joy was replaced with disappointment and fear, and the crowd dispersed. The grand room was all but empty.

The village—expecting the worst—held vigil at the palace gates.

For two days there were constant prayers, gifts, and well-wishers. The admiration and esteem the people had for her was very real, and most traveled many hours to be there.

Soft murmurs could be heard from the corridor. No music, no celebrating, and no feasting. It was a testament to exactly how precarious the situation had become.

What a difference it was from just twenty-four hours earlier.

There had always been doubt from the people that one so small and meek could carry and deliver a healthy child; now it seemed that they were correct in their belief. But no one dared to say it out loud, and it did not lessen their genuine affection and love for her.

Alaa sat just outside the chamber door. Head in his hands, overwrought with concern and despair. He never wanted this; he only wanted her. He had feared this outcome from the moment he found out she was with child. She had convinced him all would be okay.

Why had he agreed?

Laila gathered all of her strength in one last desperate attempt to focus her energy. Her body was not her own any longer. Nature had somehow taken over, and so much was out of her control.

When the urge came for her to bear down again, the midwife took a knife and cut the princess and then reached far up into her to maneuver the baby's shoulders. First one, and then the other.

Laila released a short, shallow scream as the baby was finally delivered into the world. She fell back onto her pillow, spent, as the room became filled with the sound of new life. The cry was strong, and relief consumed her.

"Is it a boy child?" she asks.

"It is a prince, Your Highness."

A contented smile spread across her weary face, and in no more than a whisper, she spoke to Hala.

"Inform His Majesty. Tell him I love him, for I cannot stay to tell him myself. Tell him to forgive me for my weakness. Thank him for making me a wife and a mother. Tell him not to be sad, for he has made my life beautiful. Let the people rejoice and do not encourage mourning, for I am nothing when compared to the future King."

And with those words and the knowledge she

had succeeded, she released her last breath. She had experienced all that she ever wanted, hoped for, or dreamed about in her short life. It was a life well lived, and to her, it was good.

Alaa, still seated, heard the new babe's cry through the door. For a moment, he wasn't sure if his ears were deceiving him. His head cocked to the side, he waited and listened. When the cry became stronger and all doubt was removed, his eyes grew wide, and he grinned.

He stood and wiped away tears with his sleeve. The feeling of relief started in his belly and worked its way up to every nerve in his body, making him shaky and lightheaded, forcing him to lean on the closest man.

Congratulations were being shouted to him from every direction, but he didn't hear them. There was only a roar in his ears and the urgent need to go be with her.

Regaining his composure, he proudly stated,

"The child is born then!"

With that, and not standing on formality, he excitedly rushed into the room.

Where instantly he knew something was wrong.

Laila's faithful maidservant crouched over his beloved, silently weeping.

At the end of the bed was a great dark crimson

puddle that seemed to grow larger by the second. His heir, swaddled and content, was in the arms of the wet nurse. But Alaa could not move. As if his feet were rooted to the floor, they would not budge. He stood and looked around, trying to absorb and understand what was clearly before his eyes. He waited for an explanation that no one was offering.

The truth of the situation was slow to come, but when it was realized, he went to her.

He takes her small, lifeless hand in his, kissing each finger. His lips peppered her palms with kisses. Oh, how he loved her hands. He allows the catastrophic pain to envelop him. Through a constricted throat, his words pour out.

"Oh Laila, dearest, please do not leave me. What shall I do without you? How will I be both mother and father to our child?"

The midwife, uncomfortable witnessing such raw emotion from a man, finally finds her voice and interrupts him.

"Your highness, you have a son."

Through tears and gritted teeth, he yells out,

"Leave us!"

They all obey, and for two days he stays with her. He will not allow anyone to wash her body or remove her for burial.

She was afraid of the dark; how could he allow

them to take her and put her in darkness forever? He will not! He will not give in.

On the third day, the King came to convince him otherwise.

After much persistence, in the end, it is agreed that she will not be put into the ground but instead placed in a tomb with a small window built into the top so that she may have sunlight. He will not have her in eternal darkness. It is the only way he will agree.

It is decided upon, and it is done.

***

Without his mother, the little prince does not thrive, and eleven days later, small and sickly, he joins her in the tomb.

Grief-stricken and plagued with guilt and emptiness, Prince Alaa lingers. Nothing could fill the void left by his love.

It seemed unfair that she was taken from him, giving birth to a son he never had the opportunity to know. He cannot come to terms with it. He cries out his anger to God and curses him for the injustice.

Sleep was fitful, and when it came, it opened a portal for her to come and visit him in his dreams. Food lost its taste; life had no meaning. He suffered with the cruelty of it all.

Each day he thought only of her. He spoke to her, smelled her scent, felt her presence around him, and longed for her touch. He wished to join her. The thought of being laid beside her and ending his torment became his comfort. It consumed him. And so, he waited impatiently for death. Just as the gardenias that Laila so lovingly tended to whilst alive had withered, so had his heart.

A year, and then two. He was not dead, but he was not living either. Only existing, and it was a slow, relentless agony.

***

Entering the third year, he was summoned to his father's bedside. The king lay dying.

Alaa sat with him in those final hours.

Looking at his father on his deathbed, he wondered when he had become so frail and old.

As his time approached, the King reached up and placed his hand on a small pouch he had tied on a leather thong around his neck. It had always been there. For as long as Alaa could remember, his father wore it. He had never asked him what it was. But then, sensing the importance of it, he became curious.

"Father, what is this you wear around your neck? It must be a dear thing for you to be clutching it so when you are about to depart from this world."

The old man struggled to breathe, took in gulps of air, and spoke slowly. He tightened his grip on the bag as if he had forgotten and then suddenly remembered again what he was holding. Choosing his words carefully and somewhat cryptically, he answered.

"Take this from around my neck. Hide it away. This was given to me by my father, who got it from his father before him. I never had need for it, as I have lived a full and charmed life. I never had need for it; I never had need."

His voice trailed off, and he seemed to doze for a moment.

Alaa did as he was told.

He untied the thong and removed the mysterious pouch from his withered digits. When the bag was in his own hands, the weight of it surprised him, which piqued his curiosity. He carefully loosened the drawstring and emptied the contents onto his lap.

He counted five identical stones in all.

Alaa selected one and held it up to the flickering candle on the bedside table. It looked strange. Smooth, glossy, and perfectly round. crystal clear and flat on one side. A singular green stripe ran down the middle, swirled with gold flakes. It seemed to have light within.

As he held it closer to the flame, beams danced all around, making everything in the room sparkle. Lending light to spaces that moments before hid in the shadows. He had never seen anything like them. They were extraordinary.

Sensing the magic they surely possessed, and for fear someone might see them, he quickly returned them back into the bag and tucked them into the sleeve of his galabaya for safekeeping.

His father, eyes still closed, spoke again.

"There is a man in Giza you must seek out who will tell you of their power. You will find him just outside of the city. He goes by the name of Sarabie. He is known as the seeing blind one. Keep these only unto yourself; guard them with your life; you mustn't tell anyone. He is the only one you can trust. My son, this will ease your suffering. If you do as I say, this will put an end to your suffering."

After a short coughing spell, the King speaks his last words. "All is not lost. Go to her.

"Alaa, go to Laila."

One

Many things define a person's life. One of the first factors is where we come from.

I don't mean geographically, although that too is a major influence. But I am speaking instead of the circumstances we are born into that are out of our control. I'm talking about the sense of worth we get from what our parents or grandparents did before us. The legacy they left behind and earned for us. That seems to be a huge factor in how we are perceived or labeled. It plays a significant part in how we ultimately view ourselves.

There is also what we do with our own lives when we venture out on our own and try to make a name for ourselves. Mistakes, trauma, and simple good or bad luck are also to be considered. But I feel when we are assessing someone's life, worth, or value, we don't take fate into account. Even when considering our own.

We have somehow romanticized the word to mean fiction, or something it isn't, giving no real thought to predestination. Maybe we each have to have an experience that convinces us of its existence. And if we come to the understanding that it does in fact exist, does that also mean that it is something unchangeable, and therefore it cannot be altered? Again, we have to experience it to such a degree that it removes any remaining doubt.

I know for me, that was the case.

But is it that there isn't constant proof of its existence all around us, or that as humans, we have to be convinced of everything these days? Anything that's out of our control, we cannot understand. And without understanding, it is easier for us to tell ourselves it doesn't exist.

It gives us a sense of power to believe we have complete control over our lives.

The truth is, the most difficult step is opening our minds to the possibilities and accepting the fact that loss of control isn't a loss at all. I am proof that once you do relinquish the mindset, unimaginable things can happen.

It has taken me some time to decide to tell my story.

I tell it now so that maybe a veil will be lifted from others' eyes as well.

Believe it or don't; it won't matter to me either way. My story isn't for skeptics. It isn't my But, for the few who open their minds to possibilities, I write this very real account of destiny, love, and universal magic just for you.

***

LONDON, England, 2019

Before I even opened my eyes, I knew I was late. The light coming in my window told me it had to be past 8:00 am. It was becoming a common occurrence as of late. God, I despise being in a rush.

Sheba was already meowing her displeasure at not having her breakfast. She was winding in and around my legs as I put on the kettle to make a quick cup of coffee and did what I needed to do to get out the door. We became tangled at my ankles, causing me to trip in my half-awake state, and I almost stepped on her.

"Okay, sweet girl, I'm sorry."

I reached down and picked her up for a quick snuggle and scratch before heading to the cupboard to see what I could find for both of us. I was out of everything.

I opened up a tin of sardines and placed the whole can on the floor. Sheba seemed pleased. I, on the other hand, would have to settle for coffee.

I decided I would grab something on the way.

I washed my face and slipped on some jeans and my favorite white button-down. Followed by a good five minutes with a lint roller trying to remove the black cat fur that seemed to cover everything I owned those days. I paused in front of the bathroom mirror long enough to brush my waist-length brown hair and tie it up into a ponytail.

After brushing my teeth and dotting on some lip gloss, I put on a pullover sweater and high-top Converse and grabbed my jacket. I decided at the last minute to leave my laptop, and I rushed out the door.

I do not know why I felt the need to hurry when I was absolutely certain that I was on my way to an appointment to be fired. I suppose I felt the need to get it over with.

Within minutes of emerging from my East London flat, it was pouring down rain.

Although I'd spent the last four years of my life in this city, it was still aggravating to me how much of my time was spent wet. I'll never get used to it— the perpetual storm dodging. There is no predicting England weather.

While waiting for the bus, I slipped on my jacket.

Not once have I ever had an umbrella when I

needed one. Not that I hadn't purchased several at that point. I had bought them, and left them, in just about every restaurant, cafe, train, and bus between my house and office over the course of my time here. At some point, I just stopped carrying one. Choosing instead to duck into doorways and under bus stop awnings when the need arose. But that day, it proved difficult since I was already about an hour late.

I arrived at my destination, drenched.

I got into the elevator and—still dripping—got out on the twelfth floor.

The office secretary, peering over her black-rimmed glasses, greeted me.

"Cate, you're late!"

"Thanks, Agnes; I wasn't aware." I said teasingly.

Agnes came from around her desk and helped me off with my jacket while handing me some tissue.

"He is in a meeting. I am to tell you to go wait in his office." She winked, and in true Texas form, she reached up and pinched my cheek. It was her way of showing support. A silent "don't worry."

Agnes, I, and the chief editor were the only Americans who worked at the newspaper. Agnes and I bonded almost instantly.

She took me under her wing the first day I started work at the Times and proved to be an invaluable friend and ally. On too many occasions to count, we sat together complaining over a shared bottle of Bourbon. All of my holidays were spent at her home with her family, and I was grateful for her. I still am; she is the mother I never had.

I grabbed a cup of coffee and a stale donut from the break room and went into the huge corner office to wait. I didn't want to sit on the expensive furnishings; I was still wet. My attention was drawn to the walls.

They were covered. I had been in that exact office dozens of times and never really looked around. It all seemed so pretentious to me. The fine furniture, sculptures, and art nouveau vibe.

I always felt as if I had traveled back to the twenties when I was in it, and I was never quite sure what to do with myself.

I think it would only have felt normal to me if I were dressed in a low-cut shift, wearing a string of pearls, holding one of those long cigarette holders, and having a cocktail.

That day I had the added discomfort of feeling like I had been summoned to the principal's office for some high school wrongdoing.

Nervous energy prompted me to walk around the room while I waited. Munching on my donut and paying attention for the first time to what was adorning every single crevice and corner. That room was a maid's worst nightmare.

One wall had the usual framed university degrees, certifications, literary awards, and college alma mater photos, strategically placed on either side of a huge plate glass window with a not-so-great view of the city. Didn't hold my interest.

The next wall was a bit better. It contained front-page photos from the London Times. To include the Queen's coronation, the royal family, political stories, and historical happenings from the past decade and beyond. There were some really great shots.

I have always been particularly fond of black-and-white photos. They seem to capture a more honest image. Although there were plenty in color, the ones that aren't are the ones I always unintentionally gravitate to.

On the wall opposite, and just above the chief's desk, was shelving. Five polished mahogany shelves that were completely saturated with stuff. Each one cluttered with travel souvenirs, family photos, and an unreasonable number of equestrian statues and ribbons. It became obvious to me that that was where the boss' true passion lay, and it was touching. After all the years I'd spent working there, perhaps I did not know him at all.

Popping the last of my breakfast into my mouth,

I moved on to the last wall. It was covered in framed photos. Not professional shots, but great nonetheless. It seemed to be a place to showcase all of the magnificent places there are in the world to visit, places in which I'd never been.

I had always planned on touring Europe once I came to the United Kingdom, but for some reason I just hadn't found the time. Most of the photos were old and included pictures of what I'd assumed were parents, grandparents, or relatives.

I lingered in front of a cluster of shots that seemed to be dedicated to Egypt. They looked to be archaeological excavation sites and displayed dates ranging from the 1930s to the 1990s. My eyes were drawn to a sepia photo.

It was a grainy pic of a man standing in front of one of the Great Pyramids of Giza. He had on trousers, a white linen shirt, and a scarf around his neck. On his head was a hat resembling the one Harrison Ford wore in *RAIDERS of The LOST ARK*. He looked to be around twenty years old.

"Catherine."

Hearing my name startled me. Hearing my *formal* name immediately put me on edge. Again, the principal's office feeling washed over me.

"Tom." I replied.

Tom is a rather large man, and he closed the gap

between us in a few swift strides. Before I could turn around, he was standing beside me, facing the wall.

He pointed to the picture I had just been observing.

"That's me, second year of college. My wife Caroline took that photo."

He paused, as if reflecting, and then he continued.

"We were both working on our archeology degrees. That was before I would have ever considered the thought of doing anything else."

In that minute, I learned two things previously unknown to me. One, that he was married, and two, that he had not been a lifelong paper-pusher. I found that not just intriguing but surprising.

"I was unaware that you were married." I said.

"I'm not. She passed away the summer after this was taken. Cancer."

I could see the pain in his face, even from my side point of view, and it somehow seemed fresh. It made me uncomfortable. As all sadness does.

"I am sorry" was all I could manage.

As quickly as his sentiment came over him, it left. I could actually feel the shift in his demeanor as he turned, headed to his desk, and had a seat behind it. He had completely regained his composure as he invited me to take my place in the "hot seat" across from him.

"Come, let's talk."

I complied.

My jeans were damp, which made the leather seat slippery, and so I sat perched on the edge.

He began,

"Listen, Cate. You know why I've asked you here today. So, let's not beat around the bush."

Before he could continue, and to my own surprise, my prepared speech started falling out of my mouth. But not in the order I had rehearsed.

"I know I haven't been a model employee, but I am a good writer. You know I am! I don't see why you would..."

He cut me off.

"Bloody hell Catherine!"

The British slang sounded funny coming from an American, especially him, and as soon as he said it, I had to suppress the urge to burst out laughing.

It is just like me to laugh when things are really serious. One of my personality defects. A nervous "tick," if you will. I prevented the laugh but not the grin. And then we were both smiling.

He paused, looked down, and then over at me. He was leaning back in his chair, fidgeting with a pen.

He uncrossed his legs, leaned forward, and put both elbows on his desk. His voice and manner were softer as he started fresh.

"You *are* a good writer. No one is disputing that. But let's face it, you are *not* a reporter. I have often wondered why in the hell you would even want to work here!"

I was rendered speechless. Not sure if I was supposed to answer that.

Was it even a question? If so, the obvious answer would have been that I preferred having a roof over my head, and I'd become addicted to being able to eat. Another one of my personality quirks—sarcasm. Thankfully, I surprised myself by keeping my mouth shut.

He leaned back and continued.

"Michael is my nephew for Christ's sake. I assure you, you can't tell me anything about him that I do not already know. I am aware of his propensities, his tastes, and his need for all things shocking or forbidden. Trust me, I've watched him destroy those closest to him his whole life. Heaven help the woman who ever truly loves him. But it doesn't change the facts."

You must have known when you jilted him what would happen. Cate, he owns the paper. I can't disregard his wishes. If you could even call them wishes. It was more of a direct order. There's no way around it—and that's that. Don't shoot the messenger."

After a heavy sigh, he sat up straight, then ran his hand through his thick, salt-and-pepper head of hair. He slipped off his glasses and made direct eye contact.

"I am prepared to give you six months' severance pay, as well as a good reference when and if you need it. Now, don't make me feel shittier about this than I already do."

Per usual, when I feel like an injustice has been done to me, my emotions revert back to that of a child, and I have to swallow hard and look away to hold back tears.

He came around the desk and sat on the front corner. He placed his hand on the armrest of my chair and spun me around a bit to face him.

"Kiddo, listen. Take my advice and look at this as a gift. Travel, take some time for yourself, and focus your energy on what you really want to do. Go find your niche and stop settling. You are a talented writer; use your talent. You might be surprised at how much you can thrive without punching a clock or having someone tell you what to write. Stop being lazy; step out of your comfort zone. A lot can happen in six months. Hell, you might surprise yourself and write the next literary masterpiece. But for me, I will never be surprised at what you accomplish. I know you have it in you. Few of us get the chance that you have been given. Do not squander this opportunity. And Catherine, that is exactly what it is—an opportunity. No matter *how* it has come about."

He reached over, grabbed a Kleenex from a box on his desk, and handed it to me.

My nose had started to run, and one rogue tear escaped my left eye. I took the tissue, wiped my nose, cleared my throat, and regained my strength as I stood to go.

"Thank you, Tom." I said as I thrust out my hand to shake.

He took my hand in both of his, and—still holding it—said,

"No thanks necessary; it has been my pleasure. On a more personal note, you know you are always welcome at my place. You look tired; if you ever need a break, the countryside would do you good."

He released my hand and went back behind his desk. I turned to go.

As I was almost to the door, he said,

"And take my umbrella from reception with you; it looks like you could use one."

And, just like that, I left the last four years of my career behind me in an ever-growing heap of personal and professional disappointment.

I nodded to Agnes on my way to the elevator. She was on the phone and covered the receiver with her hand as she mouthed for me to 'call her later.' I retrieved my jacket, and armed with my new umbrella as a parting gift, I stepped back onto the London streets. Where it had become a beautiful sunny day.

Two

It didn't look as if it would rain again any time soon, so I decided to walk home.

I remember taking the scenic route, cutting across the city by way of the Thames, so I could come to terms with the morning events. I was in desperate need of an attitude adjustment, and London is so damn beautiful that time of year. I figured the walk would do me good.

I sat for a while in an outside cafe alongside the river, watching people. Walking their dogs, jogging, strolling hand-in-hand. All seemingly without a care in the world, while I was still trying to understand how mine had just fallen apart.

When I'd had enough of my own personal pity party, I resigned myself to my fate and began tossing around ideas of what I should do next. All of my thoughts were invading my mind at the same time.

After realizing nothing was going to be resolved that day, I headed in the direction of my apartment with plans of a detour to the grocery store.

I reached into my jacket pocket to check my cell and realized it wasn't there. Of course it wasn't. I'd left it in my laptop bag that morning in my rush to go get fired.

"Dammit." I muttered to myself.

Luckily, I did have my wallet, and so I headed to the market.

After grabbing a few bags of necessities, I decided to finish my journey on the bus.

Arms loaded down, I hopped on the packed 220. Which is where I first laid eyes on him.

As I made my way to the back, a man got up to offer me his seat. And initially, I declined. But as the bus jerked forward, I dropped a bag, and apples and oranges started rolling down the aisle.

Again, he stood and said,

"Please."

He accentuated his words with a dramatic bow, sweeping his arm out in my direction, then back to the seat.

We both giggled, and that time I couldn't refuse.

This was the beginning of a pattern that would form rather quickly—my inability to refuse him. And even now, it makes me smile.

I went to set my remaining bags down in my

newly acquired seat so that I could retrieve my fruit.

He raised his flattened palm, signaling for me to stop.

"No, allow me."

He then proceeded to perform the task of collecting my produce from the floor.

It was a bit comical, this tall, good-looking guy in business attire chasing rolling fruit. Some pieces had disappeared under seats, and a few oranges had reached all of the way to the front of the bus and were resting next to the driver.

But he chased each one down and didn't stop until his mission was complete.

After returning them all back into the bag and handing it to me, he took a spot standing a couple of feet away in the disabled section. And it's then that I noticed he had a companion. Standing beside him was the cutest little white dog.

Two stops later, the seat beside mine became vacant, and with groceries in my lap, I mimicked the same arm gesture he had made to me earlier. Again, we both laughed. I scooted into the empty spot, and he took the aisle seat. His dog jumped up between us.

"Mish, no, Get down." He snapped his fingers and pointed to the floor.

After scolding the little guy, "Mish" immediately

hopped back down and lay at his feet. My new seatmate reached over my bags, extended his hand, and introduced himself.

"I'm Alaa."

"I'm Cate. And thanks."

"No problem."

I've never been any good at making polite conversation, but I tried.

"He's cute; is he a Jack Russell?"

He replied,

"Thanks, but no, he's a mutt."

I settled in and faced forward, but in my peripheral vision I could see him staring. His eyes were blazing a hole into the side of my head. I felt the intensity of his gaze long before I looked at him directly.

One thing about me: whenever I get around an attractive man, I get awkward. It is something I can't control even at thirty-one. I've never learned the proper way to address it. Which was frustrating, because at that point I'd had plenty of practice.

I turned to him, and for a moment, we just stared at one another. Our faces were mere inches apart. I felt mine starting to flush and looked away first.

He cleared his throat in what I thought was a futile attempt to disguise the fact that he felt just as awkward.

That still didn't make it any less uncomfortable.

Without another word spoken—and one stop short of my intended one—I rose to get out.

I will do anything to avoid feeling out of control in a situation, and he had a weird effect on me. With all of the calm I could muster, I tried—and failed—to exit the bus gracefully. I felt as if my legs weighed a thousand pounds each.

I looked over my shoulder as I stepped down and tripped over my own two feet, recovering just in time to prevent myself from falling face-first onto the pavement.

Once outside, I gave a last look up in the direction of his window.

He tipped his chin up and gave me a slight wave, grinning. He looked amused.

Embarrassed, but mindful of my manners concerning his kindness, as the bus pulled away, I mouthed,

"Thank you."

Still smiling, he mouthed back,

"You're welcome."

I turned and walked the four blocks to my place.

Once at home, I slipped out of my jeans and into some comfortable sweatpants. Hair went up into my usual messy bun. I put my groceries away and filled Sheba's bowl with her favorite kitty kibble. My stomach started to growl, reminding me that my only meal had been a dry donut. Even though I had just purchased groceries, after the day I'd had, I was in no mood to cook. On impulse, I grabbed my cell and decided to call my usual Chinese takeout.

I had six missed calls from Agnes, and I was not ready to recap the day to her yet. I decided to eat first.

After placing my order, I opened my laptop on my coffee table to review some of my work.

I had started and abandoned at least twenty story lines in that last year alone. I just couldn't find anything I was passionate and knowledgeable enough about to write a whole book. It seemed that all worthwhile ideas had already been taken.

An hour into reading my own crappy outlines, I'd had enough.

I felt disillusioned and depressed, and so I did what I always do when I feel that way. I went over to my extensive vinyl collection and started sorting through jazz and blues albums. It didn't take long for me to settle on Billie Holiday; she's my favorite.

In no time, the sound of her sweet, soulful voice belting out *Lady Sings the Blues'* filled my living room—somehow it seemed appropriate.

Agnes called again while I was pouring myself a glass of red, and knowing she wasn't going to give up, I answered.

"Sweetie, you didn't call me back. Are you okay?"

She always sounds panicked; that time was no different. Even when there is no obvious reason to be in a tiff, her voice just seems perpetually laced with anxiety. I have to think it is a side effect of having so many children; there's simply no other explanation.

I was still on the phone giving her my excuses when my doorbell rang. Expecting Kim's Oriental Express, I was more than taken aback by who was standing there instead.

It was the guy from the bus earlier, and he was holding my takeout.

"Agnes, can I give you a call back in a few? Someone is at my door."

I didn't wait to hear her answer before hanging up. I stood there in my doorway with my lips parted and no idea what to say. He spoke first.

"Look, I know how this appears, but let me explain."

He handed me the bag containing my lo mein and reached into the front pocket of his hoodie and pulled out my wallet.

It took a minute for it to register what was in his hand. How did he have my wallet?

"You left this in the seat on the bus. Your license was in it with your address—I came in the front door behind the delivery boy."

He spit it all out in one sentence and waited for my reply.

I was trying with everything in me to form words correctly, but my brain and mouth had forgotten how to work together to do so. While I was attempting to rectify the situation, and before I could even thank him, Sheba saw an opportunity with the open door and took it. She bolted out in a black blur down the hallway toward the stairwell. My words came readily enough then.

"Shit! Get her!" I blurted out.

Before I could finish the sentence, he had already sprung into action and was in pursuit, with his little dog running behind him.

I grabbed my wallet from my welcome mat where it had been dropped, threw it and the takeout onto my counter, and quickly followed them down the corridor.

When I caught up, he had Sheba cornered in the stairwell on the floor below. I looked over the railing.

He was crouched down, hand extended, speaking to her in a soft, easy tone. I stayed put, curious to see how it would play out. From past experience, I learned that aggressively going after her only sends her into more of a frenzy. Which makes her capture next to impossible.

The dog was going berserk, spinning around in circles and barking, until he turned to him and said something I didn't hear. Whatever he said had an immediate effect on his furry friend. He ceased barking and sat, allowing him to turn his attention back to my feline escape artist.

"Sheba, don't give me trouble, old girl. You know I won't hurt you."

Sheba pursed her nose as if sniffing the air, one leg timidly out before her, standing completely still. It was a standoff.

He got closer and lower, down on one knee, hand still extended. He spoke, alternating between English and a language I was not familiar with, in a voice as smooth as honey.

"Habibti, must we do this every time? *Tael alaa huna.* Yes, that's it, come."

To my shock and surprise, the cat, who generally hates everyone, walked right up to him and practically jumped into his arms.

Triumphantly, he headed back up the staircase, holding Sheba. She was licking his chin as he handed her over to me, and at that point I felt obligated to invite them in.

As Alaa followed me across my threshold, I asked

jokingly,

"Can I call you Al?"

"Absolutely *not.*" He said, laughing.

In an odd turn of events, shortly thereafter, I was setting my small dining room table for two while he thumbed through my record collection. I had invited a complete stranger into my home for dinner, and to this day I have to wonder: What is wrong with me?

He was studying my classic jazz section intently. He paused on a Louis Armstrong album, flipped it over, and began reading the back cover. I stopped what I was doing and tried to keep from being obvious as I observed him. My initial thoughts?

If I had had to guess his age from his looks, I would have said mid-thirties, but his mannerisms seemed much older. There was something unusual about him. Something I couldn't put my finger on. He gave an air of power; even his walk was regal somehow—aristocratic. Although he appeared down-to-earth, he radiated confidence while simultaneously seeming uncomfortable in his own clothing. He looked exotic—middle Eastern maybe? His name would say so.

Earlier I had witnessed him speak a different language, and yet he spoke English without a definitive accent—at least not one I had ever heard. I had no idea of his origins, and there was no real way to tell. I may not be a reporter, but all of my training from the previous four years was telling me there was much more to him than meets the eye.

I admit, I was intrigued.

Tact and his intimidating good looks made me hesitant to bombard him with too many questions, but I did ask him a couple of pressing ones.

"What did you say to Sheba? What language was that, and what did you mean when you asked her if she must do this every time?"

He looked up from the record and answered casually,

"I just assumed this was a habit of hers. I told her to come to me in Arabic. May I put this album on?"

"Sure." I said, and then I complimented him on his taste in music.

"Same to you; this is an outstanding jazz collection you have here. Nothing compares to the sound of jazz on vinyl. Other than live, it is the only way to hear it the way it is intended to be heard."

"I wholeheartedly agree, and I hope you like veggie lo Mein."

He replied with a sideways smile.

"It is my all-time favorite."

"Wine?" I asked, "I've only got red."

"No thanks; I don't touch the stuff. Other than

alcohol, whatever you've got will be fine."

He put Louis on and wandered around my apartment a bit, making me self-conscious. My space was neat enough but sparse.

It isn't that I don't like pretty decorations; it's just that I prefer tidy over clutter.

Other than the stolen gardenias I picked from the neighbor's shrub and kept in cups scattered about, I'd never felt the need to glam the place up.

I had had a total of three visitors the whole time I'd lived in that flat. It served its purpose, and I found it adequate and comfortable.

He eyeballed my open laptop for a moment before asking,

"What is it you do, Catherine?"

Even the way he articulated my name was strange. He drew it out and rolled the "r."

I walked over to hand him a can of Sprite.

"Up until today I worked as a writer for the London Times, and it's Cate."

He took the Sprite and didn't reply. But he raised his eyebrows, as if to ask me for more information on my last statement.

I caught myself rolling my eyes. Another bad habit of mine. In all honesty, discussing my problems with a man I'd only met a few hours prior seemed as absurd to me then as it does now. Instead, I told him that it was a long story that I would tell him some other time, and then I invited him to take his place at the table.

Before we could sit down, his phone rang. He excused himself to take the call outside in the hallway.

He returned a few minutes later with apologies. Something came up, and he had to go. But not before we quickly exchanged contact information.

"Mishmish, let's go, mate."

His faithful companion reluctantly gave up his warm place on my area rug and obediently followed. Alaa stopped at the door, turned to me, tipped an imaginary hat, and, ignoring what I said earlier pertaining to my name, said,

"Catherine."

And with that, he left.

Afterwards, I ate. I downed my glass of wine, staring at the unused plate and cutlery still sitting in front of me. I cleaned up, and within the hour I had completed my nightly routine and was in bed, but I couldn't sleep.

Instead, I lay there, recalling the details of the day. Dissecting them even more than usual. Surprisingly, my thoughts were mostly consumed with my afternoon.

I couldn't stop going over the bus ride and his visit. I kept playing the events over and over in my mind on a loop, obsessively reviewing the dialog. And then I realized why.

I was trying to remember at what point I told him Sheba's name.

I hadn't. I was absolutely sure; I never told him. He already knew.

Three

The next morning, I woke up to my phone ringing. I rolled over to check the time on my backup alarm clock that sat on my nightstand. The one I hadn't set. I'd slept until almost 12:30.

"Wow, Cate, welcome to the life of the unemployed."

I answered the phone, and the voice on the other end was none other than that of my new takeout delivery boy.

"Catherine? It's Alaa; are you okay? You sound funny. Did I catch you at a bad time?"

How would he know if I sounded strange? We had never had a phone conversation; that was the first. I hadn't even had time to save his name and number. I replied,

"Yeah, I'm okay, what's up?"

"Hey listen, I will be in the area in about an hour; can I come by? I have something I'd like to discuss with you."

Sheba started whining, jumped up, and put her

tail in my face. I couldn't think. I propped myself up on my elbow, yawned, and wiped my eyes with the back of my free hand.

"Sure, I'll be here. The code for the door is 1212. Or just let me know when you're here, and I'll buzz you in."

"Great." He said, "I'll see you in a bit."

I hung up, and our first phone conversation was history.

I swung my legs over the side of my bed and just sat there on the edge for a minute. Why did I feel so lethargic? I'd just slept for almost thirteen hours for Christ's sake.

I got up and put the kettle on, fed Sheba, and got a quick shower, and about an hour after our call, we were seated on my couch having coffee.

He started out weak in relaying to me what he wanted, seeming to struggle through small talk for about twenty minutes. Finally, he picked up his cup, raised it in the air in a "cheers" motion, and after swallowing the last of it, he set it down. He crinkled his nose, showing his displeasure at my Nescafe, and then began again. Our conversation went something like this:

Him...

"Have you ever been to Edinburgh?"
Me.

"As in, Scotland?"

Him.

"Is there another Edinburgh?"

Me...

Him...

Me.

"No, I've never been; why?"

Him.

"I have business to tend to there. I'll be there for a few days. I am driving; do you want to come with me?"

I thought about it for a minute. It wasn't like I had more exciting offers to consider.

"When?" I ask.

Him.

"We'll leave in a few hours."

Me.

"Why would I? I don't even know you. You could be a serial killer."

He chuckled, recovered, and then looked at me dead serious and said,

"You got me. I want you to come with me so that I can murder you and bury you all over the Scottish countryside. No other girl will do. But I promise to show you a great time before you meet your demise.

Now, are you in or are you out?"

I considered it for not nearly enough time to make such a decision, and then in a voice that didn't even sound like my own, and for reasons beyond my understanding, I said,

"Okay. But I'll have to find someone to watch Sheba. How much time do I have to get ready?"

He told me he'd be back at 4 pm, and as quickly as he'd arrived, he was gone.

As I was scattering clothes out onto my bed to pack, I thought about the fact that I didn't have a clue as to what he did for a living, or even his last name. I was about to put my complete trust in a total stranger. The realization of my carelessness and all-around basic stupidity astounded even myself. What was I doing? And yet—feeling that way—it never once crossed my mind to back out.

I packed some things and gave Agnes a call. She agreed to watch Sheba.

He arrived promptly at the prearranged time, and before I knew it, we were headed down the road to Agnes' house to drop her off.

When we arrived, she came out to get the pet carrier, and we met halfway up her walkway. She peered over my shoulder and saw Alaa in the driver's seat of a brand-new BMW convertible and grinned.

"Holy hell, Cate! I didn't even know you were

seeing anyone."

I handed over Sheba, who was frantically trying to escape her temporary prison. I hugged her, gave her the kibble, and told her I'd explain later.

She accepted the short explanation, responding with a wave to Alaa and commenting under her breath.

"All I'm going to say is that *I* wouldn't push him out of *my* bed."

She gave me a wink and told me not to worry; she would take care of Sheba.

"Go have a good time; you deserve this."

As she turned to go into her house, she half waved with the hand carrying the cat food and yelled out.

"Call me later, sugar!"

God, I love that woman.

***

We stopped just outside of London to fill up the car, and I watched him walk into the gas station. He was wearing blue jeans, loafers, a baby blue Oxford button-down, and a brown leather jacket. Not a hair out of place, beard meticulously groomed. I watched him hold the door for a woman coming out, and even she turned back around to check him out.

I found myself doing the same thing I have done my whole life. I started describing him in my head, the way I would if I were writing a story. And I wondered: is it just writers that do that, or does everyone?

He's tall and lean but not chiseled. His physique is more natural, "God-given." He isn't initially striking. There is something in his personality that radiates from inside out that makes him so. Dark hair, dark eyes, and dark skin give him an exotic appearance—mysterious. But it's his smile that makes him stand out...

My inner dialogue was interrupted as he got back in. He made a comment about the clouds, raised the top, and we got on the road once more.

There was no forced conversation on our journey. Both of us just enjoyed the scenery. There was no gap trying to be bridged, no emptiness trying to be filled. The comfortable silence was just *comfortable*.

I was in a car with a man I hardly knew on my way to an unknown adventure, and every single aspect of that scenario goes against who I normally am. But somehow, I was unbothered. Hell, *I was excited.*

At some point, Mishmish jumped from the back seat into my lap, and somewhere in between England and Scotland, with the sound of the car stereo and the hum of the road, we both fell asleep.

When I woke up later, the driver's seat was empty. We were parked in front of a row of shops in what looked to be a quaint little town. I put my new four-legged friend in the back seat and stretched. I wondered where we were.

A few minutes later Alaa was headed towards us with a few bags.

He opened the trunk and stowed away whatever it was he had just purchased, then popped back into the driver's seat.

"What's all that about?" I asked him.

"You'll see. "Nosy" was his reply.

He was grinning like a little boy as he handed me a convenience store flower; it was a pink and purple lily. It was the sweetest gesture, and he was adorable. I couldn't help the smile or the blush.

A few miles further, he pulled off of the main road and onto a single lane, flanked on either side by huge elm, oak, and cedar trees. We wound around thickly wooded hills for another ten minutes or so before seeing signs of civilization again.

He found a place to park on the side of the road next to an oddly placed wooden fence, and I still didn't know where we were or the purpose of our stop.

"Don't tell me," I said. "It's rope and duct tape in the mystery bags, and this is where I am going to meet my demise."

He didn't laugh. As a matter of fact, there was a tinge of hurt and indignation in his reply.

"Although I know you are saying this in jest, from my experience, there is a hint of truth in all jokes. If you feel this way, why did you agree to come?"

"I trust you; I was only kidding!" I told him. And what I find strange in that comment is that I really did *trust him*. Based on nothing, he had my complete trust.

"Then hurry up! We are running out of time."

For what we were running out of time for exactly, I did not know.

He opened my door first, then went around to the open trunk. He retrieved a backpack, put his earlier purchases inside, and then threw it over his shoulder. He took a minute to consult Google Maps, and the three of us headed off into the unknown.

After a short hike, we came upon a hill with a wide view of everything below. There, sprawled out in front of us, was a lake. Set deep in a valley surrounded by green rolling hills and mountains. Clouds parted and sunbeams struck the calm water, creating a perfect mirror image. It was picturesque. We started our way down.

My short legs were no match for his long ones, and I had to take three steps for every one of his to keep up. Mishmish was already way ahead of us at the bottom, running down the lake shore, zigzagging in and out of the water.

Alaa waited for me to catch up at the last steep incline and grabbed my hand to help me down. He paused and looked up at me. That look almost caused me to lose my footing.

In that moment, he looked familiar. I can't explain it. Overwhelming familiarity.

He stepped down, reached back up to me, placed his hands on my waist, and lifted me to the ground. I landed a few inches away from him. He smelled of leather and earth, and my stomach did a little jump—a surge of excitement.

We followed Mishmish until we came to a huge uprooted tree. It was leaning, the top almost resting on the earth, but not quite. Where the roots had been pulled from the ground, so had the dirt. It had long since been covered with grass and leaves and offered a nice place to sit.

Alaa pulled from his backpack a small disposable grill, meat, chips, and juice. In my coat pocket I happened to have apples, and right there beside a lake in the English countryside, he prepared us dinner.

After the trouble he had taken, I didn't have the heart to tell him I don't eat lamb or any red meat at all. I just ate it, and as a pesce-pollotarian, I am a bit embarrassed to admit that it was delicious.

As we finished up, the sun started to set, and all at once I understood why he was trying to rush me.

He wanted to see the sunset. Correction: he wanted *us* to see the sunset. And for good reason—it was truly one of the most beautiful displays of nature I have ever seen.

I felt as if I had been inserted into a cheesy romantic novel, and to be honest, I was enjoying every second of it. Correction:

I took out my cell phone and snapped a few pictures. He did the same, and when he wasn't looking, I took the opportunity to get one of him.

It is still one of my greatest possessions that picture of him.

It's a perfect profile shot, with the mountains, lake, and sunset behind him. The hazy glow of twilight gives him an angelic appearance—I love it.

I tossed him an apple from my stash. He took it, smiled and said,

"The infamous bus fruit. I earned this apple, but with the memories attached to it, it just seems wrong to eat it."

He sat, seeming to admire it for a minute, before taking a bite.

We ate our apples in silence while watching the sun complete its descent behind the mountains. Then we packed up and made our way back to the car in the dark, with only the flashlights on our phones.

Another two hours on the road, and we reached our final destination.

It was late, and as the car came to a stop at the end of the driveway, the headlights shone onto a beautiful little rock cottage. It was by far the most storybook scene I have ever witnessed.

He shut off the engine. The moon cast just enough light onto the house and walkway and gave it a dreamlike quality.

Mishmish jumped out and quickly relieved himself on a shrub on the way to the porch.

Alaa retrieved a key from above the door frame and opened it. I followed him in, where, just inside, he flipped on a lamp. It was more amazing inside than it was on the outside.

"Whoa! This place is spectacular! Is it an Airbnb?"

"No, it's mine." He said it nonchalantly as he put our things down and went around turning on lights.

I am sure I did not hide my surprise.

He immediately went to the fireplace and built a fire from the wood stacked on the hearth, and when it was blazing to his satisfaction, he grabbed my bag and led me to a small, neatly kept room.

It was tastefully furnished with antiques, from the bed to the washstand and everything in between. Dark, polished paneled walls, Scotch plaid drapes, and so much personality. It was perfect, except for one thing. I hadn't seen another room, and there was only one bed.

My mouth open, I turned to him to voice my concern, but he already knew what I was thinking.

"No, no, no. Don't get the wrong idea. I will take the couch; you get the bedroom."

He was smiling, not even trying to hide his amusement. I—on the other hand—was relieved.

He showed me to the bathroom, placed fresh towels on the vanity, and then left me to wash off the day.

As I undressed, I discovered the beginnings of a bruise on my waist. I looked to my other side, where there was a carbon copy. I thought back to earlier in the day when he'd helped me down from the ridge. He hadn't been rough, and he didn't grab too tightly, but there they were: bruises that perfectly matched the imprints of his hands.

I reached down with my index finger, tracing the outline of where his thumb had been—where he left his print. I felt warm inside. There was something about him leaving a mark on me that I *liked*. I placed my hand over my stomach for a second and closed my eyes, recalling his touch. I felt confused and a bit foolish thinking about the power that a complete stranger had over me, but I believe that was the second I knew. There was nothing ordinary about him—about *us*.

The cold air snapped me out of it, and I got in the shower.

Yoga pants and a t-shirt were not enough to stay warm in Scotland, and it became entirely clear to me that I hadn't packed appropriately. I was cold and shivering when I went to my room. And then I saw, laid out on the bed, a very large fluffy robe.

I was thrilled to have it and emerged with it on. I sat down in front of the fireplace to run a brush through my wet hair, hoping the location would help it dry a little. Mishmish and I had the same idea, and he lay curled up beside me.

Thinking back to that first night, it didn't feel like a first night at all.

There was a feeling of belonging. A feeling surrounding me gave me warmth and an inner calm I had never experienced. Sometimes we don't know that we are lacking anything until we experience it for the first time.

Alaa came from the kitchen with two cups of tea.

It smelled of mint and honey. He'd thought of everything.

It didn't take long between the tea and the toasty fire for my eyelids to grow heavy. I just couldn't seem to get enough sleep. I finished the cup and excused myself for the night. Avoiding for another day the inevitable questioning that comes with getting to know someone.

I fell asleep as soon as my damp head hit my pillow.

Four

While standing in the kitchen early the next morning, it occurred to me that I had gotten involved with one of those morning people I usually avoid. I've always found that part of the day unsatisfying, to say the least.

Alaa, on the other hand, seemed quite cheerful and hummed an unusual tune while he went about preparing our breakfast.

He had a small towel thrown over his shoulder, and he was making coffee in a tiny little copper pot over the gas stovetop. I had never seen coffee made like that before. It seemed time-consuming but interesting.

As if he knew what I was thinking, he said,

"Anything worth having takes time."

When he finished, he filled my cup and handed it to me, then started making his own.

I grabbed a seat at the rather large rustic dining table. It filled up most of the space allowed, with the only other furnishings on that side of the room being a small hutch and an oddly placed coat rack. As I looked around for the first time in the daylight, I was delighted.

It was an open floor plan. Essentially one big room, with furniture making the distinction between where one room ended and the other began. Uncluttered—it all seemed to be exactly where it should be—as if the furniture was built to go with the house. A small sofa, a wingback chair, a few tables, and a secretary. Everything was upholstered in the same rich dark hues, but not necessarily matching otherwise. Eclectic and charming.

The only personal items scattered about were stacks of books. Old leather-bound ones. The kind that smells like vanilla, old bird's nests, and sandalwood—the kind I adore.

He put scrambled eggs in front of me, placed a plate of buttered toast down between us, got his coffee, and had a seat.

It really is funny to me the things I have the most vivid memories of; my first sip of that coffee is one such thing. One of the most surprisingly wonderful flavors I'd ever experienced. I felt as if I had been lied to my whole life about what coffee should be.

"Why does this taste so good? What did you do to it?"

"It's Turkish coffee; it has cardamom in it. Much better than that bean water you consider java, yes?"

I should have been offended, but I wasn't. Instant coffee is pretty awful. While I sat enjoying that cup more than was reasonable, he asked,

"Where are you originally from, Catherine?"

The Q&A part of our relationship had begun, and it was too early. I swallowed my bite of toast and answered.

"The United States, more specifically, New Mexico. And you?"

Mimicking my response, he said, "Egypt, more specifically, Cairo. Why don't you work for the paper anymore?"

Good lord, I knew then I wasn't going to be able to enjoy my breakfast, or even get the chance to properly wake up, for that matter.

"It's a long, boring story, but to summarize, I met my ex-boyfriend Michael in Texas my last year of university, and he offered me a job at the London Times. He owns it by way of inheritance. I moved to the UK after I graduated four years ago. Things went south. I got fired."

"I mean, I knew long before I said anything that he was carrying on with other women; it just got to a point that everyone else knew too. His pictures, along with his 'flavors of the week,' were plastered all over social media *daily*. I couldn't do it anymore; I didn't want to do it anymore. So, I spoke up, broke up with him, and lost my job in the process. But to be honest, I wouldn't have stayed with him as long as I did if he hadn't paid off my student loans. I felt like I owed him. And that's it; the end."

He had food in front of him but didn't seem interested in eating it. Instead, he pushed his plate to the side and leaned back, allowing Mishmish to jump in his lap.

"Mishmish—interesting name. What does it mean?" I asked.

"It was my wife's crazy idea of cute, and it means apricot in Egyptian Arabic. There's a little more to it than that; I'll go into greater detail at a later time. The Egyptian humor would probably escape you now."

My stomach dropped; all I heard from that answer was "wife." I was struggling to swallow my mouthful of eggs.

"You're married?" I asked.

"Wow, Catherine, really? Is this your opinion of me? Of course, I am not married. She passed away some years ago."

Looking at him, I saw the same look on his face that I'd seen a few days before on Tom's. Again, I was uncomfortable with the obvious sadness, and again,

"I'm sorry" was all I could manage.

After a few seconds of awkward pause, I couldn't control myself anymore. As if to fill in the empty space, I started asking him a litany of questions that had been running around in my head since the night at my apartment. *He* had started it after all.

"So, you're Egyptian; does that mean you're Muslim?"

"Yes, and no." I no longer buy into organized religion. And yet, I celebrate them all. Anything that draws a person closer to God, the creator, or the source, should be celebrated."

I did not expect that answer, but I recovered quickly and fired off the next one.

"What do you do for a living as a profession?"

"I know what you meant. I'm a surgeon. But I focus more on holistic, or preventative, practices. I try to learn and promote skills that are more of a natural approach. Basically, I am a surgeon who tries to avoid performing actual surgery at all costs."

That explained the BMW and ownership of the cottage, I thought to myself. But again, his answer surprised me. Next question.

"How did you know Sheba's name? The other night, when she escaped, you called her by name. How did you know that?"

For a second, he looked lost. But only briefly.

"You yelled her name when she ran out your door. I assure you, I am not gifted with psychic abilities. Why do I feel like I am being interviewed?"

He walked over and scraped his eggs into the dog's bowl, then took both of our plates to the kitchen.

"What of your family, Catherine? Are they still back in America?"

That is always the part I hate. I despise revealing that part of my history. I answered him while bracing myself for *the look*.

"I don't have family. I was placed into foster care at a week old. I bounced around different families in my younger years, only to be sent to an orphanage in my early teens. I aged out at eighteen, and I've been on my own since. It is why it took me so long to complete my degree; I had to work odd jobs and pay my way through. Agnes is the closest thing I have to a family."

I finished speaking and, from past experience, paused to give him a chance for what I told him to register. Then, I sat waiting for *the look*.

But it didn't come. He did not give me the look of pity I'd become so accustomed to once I told anyone that part of my life.

Instead, he washed both plates, set them in the drain, and told me to go get ready. Apparently, we had a busy day ahead.

Relieved, I went and did exactly that.

***

The city of Edinburgh turned out to be only a twenty-minute car ride away and was by far the most gorgeous place I had ever seen.

Five-hundred-year-old buildings side-by-side along seemingly endless cobblestone streets. Each architectural masterpiece is unique and different from the next.

The multicolored pastel color of the buildings lent a dreamy effect to everything, as if painted by an artist in watercolor.

Gargoyles placed on the corners of ten-story gray, lacy buildings. Most with steeples or decorative shingles. It was unreal. I fell in love immediately.

Reduced to a giddy tourist from the second his little car passed the first stretch of shops. Like a child, I couldn't contain my excitement. Pointing and telling him to "look!" with every new scene laid out before me. The overall vibe of that city is beyond any expectation I had about anywhere or anything, ever.

He was overjoyed at my reaction, shown by the simple smile plastered across his face the whole time we were there.

It was cold, but otherwise, a beautiful day. He parked the car, and we got out to explore on foot.

Edinburgh Castle sits atop a hill overlooking the city, and we headed down a little narrow alleyway and started our way up. Thousands of individual handmade stones made up the ground on which we were walking, each one carefully placed like puzzle pieces. I was surprised at how much pleasure it gave me just to walk on that particular street. The royal mile is what it's called, and it was a *whole mood* in itself.

We reached the castle, and the view was astounding. Miles and miles of city and countryside could be seen. It was almost too beautiful to handle. After pictures were taken and scenery enjoyed, we walked back down and made our way through the center of town.

A Scottish man in a green Tarleton kilt was standing on the corner playing the bagpipes. The distinctive melodious whining of them echoed off of the stone and concrete buildings, amplifying it to perfection.

It invoked an unexplainable feeling deep inside of me. Something like pride or reverence. For the first time in my life, I was so overwhelmed with the beauty of something that it brought me to tears.

Embarrassed by my newly discovered weakness, I looked to him.

He was standing a few feet away, staring. Not at our surroundings, but at me.

I held his gaze for a moment. Even though he displayed no clear emotion, it was apparent that he was always boiling just under the surface. There was an intensity in his gaze, and at first it was a little intimidating. I was still trying to decide if I liked it.

The rest of the day was spent in parks, cathedrals, and catacombs.

Late in the afternoon, both of us were tired and a bit deflated after so much excitement. We found a restaurant and ordered some takeout.

While we waited, the sky became cloudy, and it started to mist.

I am not sure why I didn't find it strange when he turned to me, handed me some cash, and asked me to go down a few blocks to a specific shop and grab an umbrella for the walk back to the car. But I didn't question it. After all he had done, I was happy to oblige.

I took the money, and I headed off in that direction.

It took me a while to navigate the streets back, but when I returned, he had retrieved the car and was illegally parked in front of the restaurant waiting. He waved for me to get in.

"Did you find an umbrella?"

"Of course, I did."

As I showed him the pink umbrella I purchased, he laughed.

I wasn't sure why it was so funny to him, until he said,

"You bought pink, oh lord. This can only mean one thing. You're in love."

I protested.

"No, I assure you, *I am not!*"

It came out much more angry-sounding than I had intended, and we both burst out laughing.

Back in the cottage after our dinner, the couch and fireplace were calling my name.

I was about to stretch out beside Mishmish and relax when he told me that I should go get cleaned up because we had plans for the evening.

Reluctantly, I did as he asked.

After a quick shower, I slipped on the fuzzy robe from the night before and went to my temporary room. Where, on the bed, was a package. A large gold foil box. I paused in the doorway, looking at it, considering what it might be.

Being raised the way I was, gifts were things I only received at Christmas, and that was *if* I was lucky enough to be in the home of a family that celebrated holidays.

I felt giddy and excited.

Smiling to myself, I went in, closed the door behind me, and opened it.

Inside was the most amazing green satin dress I had ever seen. I sat there with it in my hands for a moment, appreciating the feel of the cool, silky fabric. I removed it completely from the tissue paper, walked over to the full-length oval mirror standing in the corner, and held it against my body. It looked as though it would fit.

I took the towel from my hair and ran my fingers through it. Forgoing the normal bun or ponytail, I chose to leave it down instead.

I slipped into the dress, and after a bit of a struggle, managed to zip up the back. It was indeed a perfect fit.

I decided if ever a dress deserved a bit of mascara and lipstick, it was that one. I took a few extra minutes to apply it, and when I was finished, I stood in front of the mirror again.

That time, my reflection was almost unrecognizable. I was satisfied with what I saw.

The dress was avocado in color, an almost exact match to my eyes. It went perfectly with my olive skin tone, giving me a healthier glow. It was simple and elegant, knee-length, scoop neck, and long sleeves. It reminded me of a classic 1950s cocktail dress. The style brought out the best of my petite 5'2" frame. It clung in all of the right places and looked as if it were tailor-made for me.

I took notice of my own facial features with makeup in the mirror. Suppressing my normal tendency to be overly critical concerning my looks, I thought that I looked pretty. I felt pretty, and I went to see if he felt the same way. For some reason, all of a sudden, that had become important to me.

As I came down the hall in my bare feet, Alaa was standing inside the entrance leading to the living area, looking devilishly handsome. Dressed in black slacks and a starched white button-down. He was leaning against the wall, and in his hands, he held a pair of simple black heels. I reached for them.

"I am assuming these are for me?"

He responded,

"My God, you are stunning."

With that statement, I felt like a bowl of Jell-O. I could hardly breathe or speak. I thanked him, then took the shoes and sat down to try them on. They too fit perfectly, and he looked relieved.

"How did you know my size?"

"I guessed, but just so you know, I got a size larger and smaller in both shoes and dress just in case." He laughed nervously.

"Did you?"

"No, I am kidding. I only got these; I'm just lucky, I guess."

When did you have time to do this? I asked him.

"Catherine, do you really think if I needed an umbrella, I would send my guest to go get it? I called a friend of mine earlier who owns a women's specialty shop. All I had to do was tell her what I wanted and in what size, and then go pick it up. The most difficult part was finding something to occupy you while I did. Are you pleased?"

"That depends. Are *you* pleased?" I asked.

"Pleased nowhere *near* describes what I am. Shall we go?"

He helped me with my coat, and again, we headed to an unknown destination.

That time, I didn't care where we were going. I knew, as long as I was with him, I would be happy no matter where we ended up.

JAMIE LEE CARRIE

Five

I could hear that the place was busy even before we reached the bottom of the narrow staircase leading in. We stopped briefly in front of the hostess stand, and he paid them for our entry.

The sound of glasses clinking and people talking was reminiscent of a cocktail party. It was a low roar, rather than a loud modern-day club. We made our way through the double doors.

The room was pie-shaped, being wider at the entry. Along one wall were six booths, with only about nine tables spaced a few feet apart in the middle. With no bright and intrusive lighting, there were lit candles on each table, giving it an intimate, warm feeling. A bar ran along the other wall, and at the very end was a small stage. Above it there was a neon sign that simply said, **JAZZ**. It had the old forbidden "cotton club" vibe. It was quaint and romantic, and I couldn't stop smiling.

The place was packed with no available place to sit, but I didn't mind. It isn't often I wear a dress, and I felt like it would have been a waste if we were sitting in a dark corner somewhere. We found a place near the bar to stand just as the musicians took the stage.

They did a short introduction, and within a few minutes, the four of them were filling the room with one of my favorite sounds in the whole world. Piano, drums, saxophone, and double bass.

It's all they needed to create magic, and I was in heaven. Apparently, he was too. All worry or concern that he normally wore on his face was gone. His usual serious demeanor was replaced with a more festive, relaxed one. And, just like Tom's cluttered office shelves, I think I discovered his passion.

After the first set, a booth opened up, and we claimed it. Once seated, I had his complete attention. The ease of conversation between us was surprising to me. I felt so comfortable.

It was more than that, though; I had a sense of belonging. Whether it was the feeling of belonging to him or to the moment was unclear. I just knew for then; I was where I should be.

The band took the stage again, and I was happy to lose him to the entertainment.

Watching him enjoy that music was a whole different level of joy. He was lost in it, and before long, I was lost watching him.

It really was a perfect evening, and we stayed for the last song. It wasn't until the lights went up and he helped me into my coat that I realized how exhausted I was.

I wasn't sure if it was the effect of the wine I drank or all of the excitement of the day. All I knew was that I was worn out and ready to go home. But I felt blissfully happy.

As we re-entered the night air, it had gone from chilly to absolutely freezing. I turned my coat collar up against the wind, but with what I was wearing, it didn't do much to help. He slipped his arm around my waist, pulled me into a sideways hug, and we walked the cobblestone streets to the car.

By the time we got to the house, my head was pounding.

I slipped off my heels and sat down on the couch while Alaa rekindled the fire. He went to the kitchen and came back with two cups of cocoa. Both of us mesmerized by the flames and digesting the day, we enjoyed them in silence.

The clock on the mantle said 1:00 am when I rose to go to bed. As much as I didn't want the day to end, I needed to lie down.

He stood when I did, and before I could say good night, he stepped closer, put his arms around my waist, and pulled me to him. We lingered in an embrace, with my cheek resting on his chest. He loosened his arms enough to look down at me.

His eyes seemed to be searching mine, questioning. But I was confused as to what they were asking.

He put his index finger under my chin and tilted my head back, his lips hovering, as if trying to decide what to do or analyzing the way to do it. I don't know the reason; I only know it created an excitement and anticipation inside of me that I had never known.

When he did finally kiss me, he did it passionately and completely.

My head was swimming. I felt strange, as though I was disconnected from everything around me—like a dream. But then he abruptly stopped.

"Catherine, why are you so hot? I mean, you are burning up!"

He pulled away and placed the top of his hand along my cheek and then his palm across my forehead.

"You're sick; you've got a fever. You had to have known; why didn't you say something?"

Not the way I had envisioned our first kiss, but there it was.

"I didn't realize I had a fever, just a headache." I responded, still in my dream state.

The look on his face immediately changed to concern as he took my hand and led me to the bedroom. He turned on the lights and turned down the quilt.

"Get changed and get into bed; I'll be right back."

I didn't have the energy or desire to argue, and within a few minutes, I was in my nightclothes and under the covers.

He came back with a glass of water and two Panadols. I took them, curled up into the covers, and with the memories of our last two days on my mind, I drifted off into a fitful slumber.

I woke up sometime in the night.

The room was completely dark when I opened my eyes. My body ached, and I was cold, shivering. I had the strangest feeling I was not alone.

I lay for a moment on my side, listening. I heard soft breathing and realized he was sleeping next to me. As if he felt me awake, his arms encircled me and pulled me closer. He buried his nose into the back of my neck and breathed in deeply. I scooted closer to him. Nestling perfectly into the crook of his body, I drifted back off to sleep.

***

With the morning light, I felt better.

I rolled over to see that I was alone. I slipped on the robe and went out into the living room. Alaa was dressed in a dark blue business suit, getting papers and necessary items into a briefcase.

"Good morning, how do you feel?"

"Better, thank you."

"Yeah, your fever broke a few hours ago. Listen, I want you to take it easy today. There is coffee in the thermos on the counter, some soup in the cabinet if you get hungry, and juice in the fridge. I have to go, but I'll be back in a few hours. I'll bring something more substantial when I come. I'd prefer you didn't do anything strenuous, but if you do decide to walk or go explore, please take Mishmish with you. He knows these woods better than I do, and he has a GPS on his collar. Just in case you get lost and can't find your way back, I could find you. If you're well enough to travel later, we need to head back to London. I need to return the rental car in the morning."

"That's not your car?" I said, surprised.

He smiled.

"No, my Volkswagen is in the shop for routine maintenance."

He came to me, kissed me on the forehead, and grabbed his keys. After a last-minute pat-down of himself and his breast pockets, he paused at the door.

"Try to get some rest; call me if you need anything. I'll see you soon."

And then he left.

I went to the kitchen, poured myself a cup of coffee, and sat down with my cellphone to check messages and emails. Nothing pressing.

Still tired and weak, I opted to stay in my pajamas. I stoked the fire and noticed for the first time, a decorative brass box on the mantle. It was unique. I picked it up to get a closer look.

It wasn't large, but surprisingly heavy. On the lid were etched leaves, ferns, berries, and a small bird in the upper right corner, with smaller ones on the sides. Four legs resembling old English wood carvings held it up, and there was a keyhole in the front. It was locked. I placed it back onto the mantle and lazily strolled around the room.

His books were amazing examples of classic literary works. Moby Dick, David Copperfield, and Treasure Island, to name a few. I came across a copy of The Good Earth, opened the cover, and saw that it was a second edition. I was more than mildly excited. I lifted it to my nose and inhaled the wonderful book aroma before closing it and setting it back onto the shelf. He has exquisite taste in literature.

After seeking out and methodically reading the front cover of every single book in the room, I wandered over to his desk.

I didn't mean to be snooping, but that is exactly what I found myself doing. It seemed that I couldn't help myself. I wasn't even going to try.

The three top drawers above the desk were filled with the normal stuff. Pens, paper clips, rubber bands, and envelopes. The top drawer, below the desk, was a bit more interesting.

First and foremost, there was a lanyard with his hospital identification card attached. Across the top, the *ROYAL LONDON HOSPITAL.* I picked it up and looked at his picture; under it said, *DR. ALAA SAIED ATTIA.* I read it out loud a few times, slowly pronouncing each syllable of his name. I decided that I liked it. I put it back where I found it.

A large leather folder occupied the other side of the drawer. The folder itself was thick, and a tightly braided cord went around the width of it, keeping it closed. I took it out and sat down at the little desk.

Inside were a few sheets of paper.

The first page looked like parchment or something I wasn't familiar with. It was tattered, dark in spots, and covered from top to bottom, front and back, in artistic black Arabic script. The second sheet, although a little worn, was normal enough and handwritten in English. And so, I began to read:

My mind is cluttered; my memories are flooded.

Mental pictures and recollections that will not ever leave me in complete peace.

I am never alone with my thoughts.

You are my constant companion. You linger.

The shadow of your essence always seems to be just over my shoulder.

Whispering into my ear,

Constructing visions in my mind's eye.

Painting vivid portraits of tantalizing scenes,

Fantasies yet to be played out.

At any given time, you surprise me with your touch, your scent, your voice, or your laugh.

You visit me, without being in my presence.

At times, permeating my dreams.

Your hidden emotions, our secrets, dance with me.

The most satisfying of dances, in which you are undeniably and wholeheartedly felt.

An invisible force.

Your hand in mine is a tender, gentle direction, leading me towards the unknown.

Each occasion is completely new, and yet, deliciously familiar.

One touch, one look, and I can do nothing but forfeit.

My body willingly succumbs.

Underlying joy and excitement heightened when considering the realm of possibilities.

I marvel at the sheer pleasure in recalling the feeling of your fingertips as they run along the contour of my hips or back.

Feathered, unhurried strokes on the inside of my thigh.

Skillfully tearing down all apprehension, modesty, or resistance I might have.

Neither nervousness nor mistrust has a place in our togetherness.

And so, you effortlessly do away with them...

Slay them in their tracks, and discard them somewhere out of reach and view.

The warmth of your breath on my neck.

Your sweet searching lips on mine; your tongue exploring my mouth.

The strength in your unwavering resolve to know all of me.

Unrelenting in its honesty.

The sincere and tangible result of yearning.

I find myself in perpetual limbo.

Waiting for the moment when you enter me, and we gasp in unison.

The real unspoken promise to find myself lost in your

world;

The perfect world that you nurture and protectively carry inside of you.

I thought I was done with this part of my life.

The need to feel someone's skin closely pressed against mine,

The hunger for one fellow soul's touch,

And yet, here it is.

So very real.

Even now, I am flushed.

It isn't stable or sure.

It's electric and satisfying.

Questions that I don't ever want to find the answers for.

A solid assurance that I will always keep looking.

I do not ever want to be satisfied.

Taste, touch, feel, absorb, merge, and exist.

Mental and physical union, reckless and catastrophic in its beauty.

Delving into something I can only imagine the depth of.

Flying too high, going too deep.

Insatiable desire and passion, fueled by the drive to just go around the next corner, a little more.

Please, just a little more.

Always challenging me.

Pushing the boundaries of what is considered possible or acceptable.

My heart and my body open wider than I ever imagined they could.

I don't care.

I do not care to entertain my mind with the idea that there isn't any more.

The only thing that is absolute is my need to know, without a doubt, that there is no end to be reached.

To avoid its demise.

The death of our familiarity; of likeness, friendship, and adventure.

The death of a dream of perfect erotic bliss.

I will entertain no thought or scenario that puts an end to this.

For now, you are mine.

The rest just seems unimportant.

I keep you tucked away. You live deep inside.

You have a home in my heart.

Revealed only in the way I smile at the thought of you throughout my day.

Shown only in the way I crave you, the way I want you, and the way that I silently need you.

~Ester

Wow, *just WOW.*

When I finished, I found that tears were sliding down my face.

I also found that I felt a very real tinge of jealousy. They had to be the words of a past lover.

Following that page was the most modern paper in the group. It was a lined piece from a spiral notebook. Again, it was written in English, and I couldn't stop...

I lay with my head on your chest.

My arm draped across your body.

My hand lightly strokes your bare skin.

Tender reciprocation.

The scent of you surrounds me.

Filling my nostrils and making me calm.

Enveloping me.

The invisible part of you,

Somehow creating more comfort.

Listening to your voice as it vibrates against my cheek is a treat for all of the senses, not just my ears.

Tickling me from head to toe, as if I am a harp, being expertly played;

Strummed and plucked until it settles on one

long note.

The sound of you pauses and collects deep into my center.

You play my heartstrings perfectly.

Sleepily, I reach up to stroke your hair.

Soft curls wind around my thumb and forefinger.

You kiss me on the top of my head; it is a certain kind of bliss.

This feeling of belonging, defying logic, is euphoric.

As we share the same space,

My soul entwines with yours, without direction or intent.

Wrapped up in each other is my favorite place to be.

Without looking up, or even opening my eyes, I enjoy you—all of you.

You are my safe place.

My soft landing, my other half,

the reflection of my passions, wants, needs, and desires.

The better part of me.

Even when alone,

I vibrate to the sound of you.

My mind recalls your voice in detail.

Although I am never quite whole in your absence,
You're never really gone, are you

-Lysette

I placed all of the pages back into the folder and tied it exactly like I'd found it.

As I was putting it back in the drawer, I spotted the edge of something shiny. I reached into the corner and pulled out a small skeleton key. I knew immediately that it went to the box on the mantle.

I retrieved the box and opened it.

Inside were two wedding bands. One tiny, the other obviously a man's ring. Silver and beautifully crafted, with gold inlay along the middle of both.

The only other thing in the box was a gemstone. One in which I had never seen anything like.

It was a bit larger than an average-sized sand dollar. Sliced through the crystal-clear center were gold flakes swirled around a brilliant green stripe. I held it in my hand for a moment. It felt warm, not cold like one would expect. A ray of light streamed from the window, reflected from the stone, and sprays of glitter splashed across the ceiling. It was fascinating, and I was mesmerized.

Not really sure why I did what I did next, but I

retrieved my phone and snapped a quick picture of it. Then, I placed it back in the box along with the rings, secured it, and put the key back into the drawer.

I spent the next few hours thinking about both the writing on those pages and the contents of that box.

Six

Having been raised in the United States, I always felt that Americans were hypersexual. I mean, from my impression, nothing compares to the United Kingdom, but they are just the same.

And although I have never had any real interest in romantic entanglements or sex, I realized pretty young that it was going to have to be something I learned. I was living in a world that looked at females as objects of sexuality. Personal experience reiterated that fact, especially while in college.

As a teenager, I approached the subject of sex as more of an educational endeavor. Even if I didn't want it the way I felt others did, I needed to find out what it was about and, at the very least, become proficient in the act.

My first-time experiencing intercourse I was fifteen, and I couldn't understand what all the hype was about. Once was enough for me to decide to put off boys for a while. I tried again in my early twenties, with the same results, and again later with

Michael while at university. Each occasion left me feeling emptier and more inadequate.

People acted as if it should be enjoyable. I could see how it would be for men, but for me it had never been a positive experience.

Which is why it was so damn confusing that I couldn't get the words from those pages out of my mind. Not just the letters, but also the evolving fantasies that had manifested and continually played in my mind about Alaa since I read them.

Those women enjoyed him. They wanted him to touch them, and more than that, they loved him for it. Something I couldn't seem to wrap my head around.

It created a need in me to experience him that way. It contradicted my feelings about the subject and created space for doubt. It left me with the impression that maybe I was the problem. Maybe I just wasn't any good at it.

Alaa returned early that afternoon, just as he said he would.

After the morning I'd spent snooping and basically disregarding his privacy, I felt a little more than guilty. I wondered if it showed. Guilt has a funny way of making a person feel more transparent than they are comfortable with. For me that day, it was especially the case.

I found myself watching him. Taking into account the small things that I had ignored the days previous. The way he walked, spoke, his mannerisms or personality traits that would give me an insight into what type of lover he would be, or why the authors of those pages were so enraptured with him. What exactly did **he** possess, if anything, that would make him different from any other men I 'd known?

My mind was obsessing, and it made it difficult to look him directly in the eyes without blushing.

He, on the other hand, seemed different. Distant, preoccupied, and quiet. I wasn't sure what had changed, only that something had.

My detachment game had long since been perfected, and hiding my feelings had become second nature. And so, I mirrored him.

We had an early dinner, tidied the cottage, cleaned the fireplace, and loaded the car. All the while, I felt on edge.

I wasn't sure why I felt that way then, but now I realize that I was waiting for him to show me the side of him that I'd experienced the night before. I'd only seen a glimpse, and I craved more.

The drive back to London, we barely spoke.

The longer we went with the obvious distance between us, the more confused I felt. I didn't understand. I had to consider that maybe I had done something wrong, something he was upset about. Was it possible he knew I had looked through his personal things? I wasn't sure.

On the last stretch of highway leading into the city, there was a loud pop that seemed to come from the right front tire. We coasted slowly down the exit and limped into the first parking lot we came to. Sure enough, it was flat.

To make matters worse, the sky opened up and it started to pour down rain. We sat in the car waiting for it to subside long enough for him to change the tire.

My apartment was on the other side of the city, and although I could have taken public transport to get there, it was late, and I didn't want to leave him to deal with the rental.

When I asked him where he lived, he explained that he lived in a shared flat near the hospital with a few other doctors. It, too, was far.

After a few calls to roadside assistance and the rental company, plans were made for the car to be picked up the next morning. Which left us sitting there, trying to decide the best course of action while waiting for the storm to pass.

Mishmish was sitting in my lap, shaking and whining while the sky dumped so much water that we could barely see out the window. Wave after wave of thunder, lightning, and then hail.

Eventually, I spoke up. I had decided to take the tube back to my place.

He was staring out the front windshield with a blank expression. His coldness seemed borderline psychotic, and frankly, it was driving me insane. After hours of short, dry answers, it surprised me for him to say what he said in response.

"Catherine, please don't leave. Not tonight. There is a hotel two blocks from here; spend the night with me."

I knew what he was asking. He was asking me to sleep with him, and if I was confused before, I was beyond confused after his request and told him,

"After the way you have been acting, are you sure you want that?"

And then, for reasons unclear to me even now, I started to cry. I turned and faced the window.

"Look at me, Catherine. Turn around and look at me, please."

I wiped my eyes on the sleeve of my coat, then turned to face him. He reached out and took my hand in his, raised it to his lips, and kissed it, lingering over my fingers with his eyes closed.

When he opened them, he looked at me in a way that hurt me to witness. There was some unknown source of torment. A look of pain that I had never seen on anyone's face before.

"I am sorry; I wish I could explain in a way that you would understand. But I can't. All I can tell you is that I need you to say okay. I need you to be with me tonight. Please say yes."

My words wouldn't come; they seemed to be stuck in my throat. I nodded my agreement.

When the rain let up, we grabbed our bags and made a dash for it. staying close to buildings until we got to the hotel.

It appeared that he had a previously established rapport with the young man at the front desk, and we were in our room in no time. We were shivering and wet, Mishmish included.

The hotel was an old Victorian-style one, with a large canopy bed, small kitchenette, and full bathroom, complete with a ball-and-claw bathtub. It was beautiful.

I walked around looking at things, touching the silk bedspread and velvet curtains, then settling in front of the window to watch the rain. We were on the top floor, and the view was amazing.

I stood there, holding my own arms, dripping on the carpet, and staring out the window.

He brought me a towel, and I tried to spot-dry my hair while he made us tea. I was trying not to appear nervous. And it was working until he came from behind to put his arms around me, and I jumped. It was a reflex from years of protecting myself that way.

For a few minutes, we just stood together in front of the window, watching the storm. I leaned against his chest, feeling him solid and warm behind me. It started to calm down. I sensed that there was no rush, and it was soothing.

There is nothing about that night that has escaped my memory. From the way he silently led me to the bed to the way he gently removed my clothing, piece by piece. To the way he tenderly touched my body. Pausing and expressing concern over the bruises on my waistline created by his hands a few days earlier. Exploring me slowly and methodically.

It was as if I had never been touched before, and I realize now—in all actuality—I really hadn't been until then. Each caress and every kiss were savored in a way I cannot describe accurately in words.

It felt as if he could read my mind, knowing exactly what to do and when to do it. The only description to come to mind would be "ecstasy," but it still somehow lacks accuracy. Sometimes the depth of feeling just can't be translated.

I understood immediately that that was how sex was supposed to be experienced.

All of a sudden, I felt cheated somehow. Shortchanged for all of the years I went without it—without him.

The letters I'd read made sense to me, and I felt hurt that he had been loved the way I felt I loved him then. Those other women knew him the same way I did. They knew him first, and I didn't like it.

Just before sunrise, we lounged in the bathtub together. I never wanted it to end. I wanted to freeze time and remain with him in that hotel room, making love for the rest of my life.

It was light outside, and we were both exhausted when we finally climbed under the covers. I lay with my head on his chest, and after a long pause in movement, I thought he had dozed, but he started to speak.

"Catherine, I want to tell you a story. I need you to promise to listen without a word until I am finished. I will answer any questions you have then."

I agreed, and sleepily, I listened as he told me a story.

It was a story like no other, and after eventual acceptance, it would shake my beliefs and somehow blur the line between what I knew to be real and what was not. A story that would be the beginning of a journey to understanding this life, for the rest of my life. It's an understatement to say that I was unprepared.

He began.

"Long ago, there was a prince…"

He shared a story of the life of a young Egyptian prince born in the late 1700s and an arranged marriage. An eventual love that was all-consuming and pure. Of a difficult pregnancy, an impossible birth, and the death of both mother and child. He told me of unimaginable grief and pain and a special tomb built into the side of a cliff in Cairo. The death of a king and of an inheritance of five magic stones. He relayed the story with so much passion and sentiment. Choosing each word as if to paint a picture that would leave no doubt on any detail. It was a beautiful story.

When he stopped, I was unclear on exactly why he had told me the tale. I lay there thinking of it all. But in the end, I was confused. Not sure of the purpose behind the hour he had just spent relaying it. Until he added a final detail.

"Catherine, this is my story. I am here because of one of those stones."

Okay, let's stop right here. Before you judge me on my response, I want you to consider what your own response would be if a man you had just spent three blissful days with told you something like that.

Slowly, an anger like I have never known spread

through me. I pulled away from him, rolled over onto my back, and stared at the ceiling. I started to shake, and for a minute, I couldn't think straight.

I had given my time to—and started to care for—a complete *madman*! What is wrong with me?

What do you say to something like that?

For me, when I realized he was serious, I couldn't speak at all. I felt foolish that I had let him seduce me.

Mad at my own naivety, I lay there and kept my mouth shut.

Alaa, sensing my anger and disbelief, got up and went over to his bag. He retrieved something out of the side pocket. He came around to my side of the bed and held out his palm. I sat up, turned on the lamp from the bedside table, and focused my eyes on what he was holding. In his hand were two medallions and a bracelet of some kind.

I reached out and took one, looking at it for a moment. On close inspection, it was a disk much like one placed on the collar of a pet. The first one I chose simply said *"Sheba"* in a rolling script. I sat up completely and reached for the other one. Again, but in block letters, it was inscribed with "Sheba." I picked up the bracelet last and realized it wasn't a bracelet at all. It was a collar, and the writing on it was in Arabic. He was quick to tell me that it too, translated to *Sheba*. I looked up at him, still speechless.

"You found her, didn't you? She was a stray who made her way in your window or followed you home from work one day, am I right? Catherine, she finds you in every lifetime, and for reasons I don't understand myself, you always name her *Sheba*."

At that point I wasn't just mad; I was livid, and my lack of sleep made it worse.

What had I gotten myself into? How long had he studied me? Followed me or obsessed over me to come up with this elaborate story and to know my cat?

I immediately got up and started to dress. I felt as if a cold bucket of water had been dumped over my head. How stupid could I be?

"I want to go home." Was all I could say.

"Catherine, I know this is hard to believe, but surely there is something inside of you that knows I am telling the truth."

"Why? Why would you do this? Are you sick? I want to go home." I said as I went about the room collecting my things and suppressing the urge to run out the door and never look back.

When we were both dressed and packed, we silently started the walk to the train station.

An hour later I was a bit calmer, but I was trying

with everything in me to put what he had told me out of my mind. To pretend it didn't happen. He hadn't just revealed to me that he was quite possibly a delusional, crazy stalker.

Halfway to the station, it started to rain harder, and we ducked into a coffee shop. When we came out, it had let up a little, and so we sat just outside the shop.

I have said before that the things I randomly remember about any given event in my life are strange.

That day, I recall that we sat on a bench and shared trivial conversation. He held the umbrella over me as I ate a cinnamon roll, and Mishmish chased pigeons. He seemed to become a more serious, milder version of himself.

I wanted us back to the way we were before. I wanted to erase everything from that morning. So, I did what I do best. I ignored the biggest red flag I had ever experienced. It was easier that way.

Sensing my inability to grasp and accept what he had told me; he seemed to put it behind him as well. Acting as if everything was normal and not speaking of it again.

Thinking back to that moment and knowing what I know now, I do not know how he did it. It must have been soul-crushing.

We enjoyed what I assumed was the last hour we would ever have together, and though my heart was breaking, I showed no outward appearance that_it was. We talked and laughed, and when it was time for us both to catch our trains, we hugged, said our good-byes, and went our separate ways.

I went back to my world, and he went back to his.

Well—*sort of.*

Seven

By the time I made it back to my apartment, I was beyond exhausted. It was surprising how badly my legs and back ached, and a slight fever had returned.

After a quick conversation to make plans for Sheba's return the following day, I slipped into sweatpants and a t-shirt and lay down. I was asleep before I could rehash any more of the day. I was physically, emotionally, and mentally spent. And so, I just slept.

The next morning, I opened the door for Agnes, filled up Sheba's bowl with food, took two Ibuprofens, and went straight back to bed. For three days I slept almost around the clock.

On the fourth day, I felt a bit better, and I moved to the couch. For a few days I spent my time wandering around my apartment. Still weak, but restless.

In my mind, I slowly started to revisit the time with Alaa. I must have thought about what he told me a million times over those next few weeks.

So, what if Sheba had been a stray who climbed into my window from my balcony one night? There must be a million cat owners who acquired their pets that way. It didn't prove anything.

A week went by, and then two. And then four. Those were the longest weeks of my life. Trying to occupy my time was next to impossible, but any downtime opened the door to thoughts of him, and so I started trying to stay busy.

Five weeks after our rendezvous in the hotel, I still hadn't heard from him. My own mind was a genuine source of crippling chaos. It wasn't just the story I kept thinking about; Alaa had taken up an exorbitant amount of my mental space rent-free.

I missed him so much I was rendered useless. If he was in fact an obsessed stalker, he wasn't a very good one. For whatever reason, he stayed away.

I was walking around in a depressed bubble. Most days I stayed in my pajamas and ordered takeout. I didn't work or have anyone to answer to, no schedule to keep, and no desire to socialize, even if I'd had anyone to socialize with. I had gotten thin, and I was a mess.

Thanksgiving came and went that year, without my usual enthusiasm. I spent it with Agnes and her family, of course, but my mind was preoccupied. Something that she noticed immediately.

She voiced her concern about my appearance and all-around mental state. I assured her I was fine, but her experience as a mother gave her some strange superhuman abilities to see right through me.

I considered telling her what was going on, but let's face it. The story was a bit more than odd, and I wasn't sure she would even believe me.

At the least, I knew she would feel the same way I had, and I didn't want her to worry that I had gotten involved with a crazy man. I returned to my life of performing the bare minimum concerning survival and just tried to move on.

I took an exorbitant number of walks through London. Not just to get out of the house, but looking back, I think I held out hope that I would somehow run into Alaa along the way.

I took the 220 dozens of times those weeks, always searching for his face in a crowd. Anytime I saw a dog, I took notice. And yet, not one time did I ever consider picking up the phone and calling him.

I perpetuated my own misery, and it was getting ridiculous.

Then the day came when I'd had enough.

If it weren't for my need for a change of scenery, I'm not sure I would have done it. But, on an especially bad day, I called Tom. Four hours later, Sheba and I were on a train headed to his country home.

It was on that visit that my life took an unexpected turn.

We arrived late, and Tom picked us up at the station. Sensing that I wasn't in the best place, he didn't pressure me. He simply let me be.

For the next week, I just lounged around his house. We settled into a routine of existing side-by-side when he was home, but never really speaking. I fished in his lake and helped him tend his garden. I spent afternoons watching him train his horses, and on the prettiest evenings, we saddled a couple up and took lazy rides around the countryside.

Rest, company, and good food. It worked magic, and physically, I felt like a new person. He was such a good friend to me—steady and consistent with his silent support.

And yet, I still couldn't get Alaa out of my mind.

I mulled over every single detail of what he'd told me. At some point, I think I started to accept it in an odd way. At least, it didn't shock me the way it had in the beginning.

Thinking I might be going crazy, one night I confided in Tom. He had earned my trust.

We were sitting by the fire in his den; he was reading, and Sheba and I were curled up on his couch, staring through the television.

I began by telling him how I'd met Alaa and the days leading up to the "story." I skipped over anything too personal, but in the end, I relayed the tale exactly as it had been told to me. I also told him about the collar and tags.

He was leaning back in his chair, listening intently. He seemed to hang on to my every word with sincere interest. When I was finished, I sat looking at him, trying to see possible signs of what he might think. His behavior was not what I expected.

In the beginning, there was no reaction at all; he just stared at me for a bit. Wordless.

Then he removed his glasses, closed his book, and got up. He walked across the room and started rummaging through a drawer in his desk. When he couldn't find what he was looking for, he went to the next, and then the next. Until eventually, from the last bottom drawer, he pulled out a manila envelope.

He sifted through a few papers until he found one with a photo paper-clipped to it. His glasses went back on, and he came over. He took a seat beside me, and with the strangest look I've seen to date on anyone's face, he handed me the photo.

I found myself staring at a black-and-white picture. Thick, as if on cardboard—grainy and very old. The quality couldn't have been worse.

It was a photograph of a petite woman with large almond eyes. She was seated on the arm end of what appeared to be a chaise lounge, and even though her face was half covered with a veil, it did not hide her obvious beauty. Standing beside her was a man in a long dress. The kind I've seen Middle Eastern men wear. I have since learned that they are called galabaya. Something about him caught my attention.

It was too unclear to see any details—and lately my eyesight hadn't been the best—but I couldn't stop staring at it.

While I was looking at the picture, Tom was studying my reaction. He got up and retrieved a magnifying glass from beside his easy chair and handed it to me.

When I placed the glass over the picture, I gasped. It was perfectly clear who was staring back at me. That man looked exactly like Alaa.

I couldn't catch my breath.

"Is it him?" Tom asked.

He waited a second and repeated louder,

"Cate, *IS IT HIM?*"

I wasn't sure I understood the question. I heard myself murmur.

"I, I... what? How could it be?"

I turned the photo over. Scribbled on the back was one simple line.

PRINCE ALAA ATTIA HASSAN AND WIFE LAILA 1799.

"Tom, surely you aren't trying to tell me what I think you are. This cannot be possible. You need to explain what is going on for Christ's sake!"

Tom tilted his head back and rubbed his eyes with his thumb and index finger, as if he were digging into the sockets. He stopped, leaned back on the couch, and just stared at the ceiling for what seemed like forever before he spoke.

"Cate, let's go put on a pot of coffee; we have a lot to discuss."

I followed him to the kitchen, and an hour later I was still seated at his island.

He'd emptied the contents of the folder and had the pages spread out. He was excited but hadn't said much to make sense yet. He was flipping through pages, removing each sheet one at a time, and putting them in some kind of order that only he would understand. I patiently sat drinking my coffee and watching him.

Periodically, he would say, "Just a minute." and hold up his finger.

Or "be patient, it's coming."

I got the distinct impression he would have said

those things out loud even if I hadn't been in the room. He was in his own little world. And then he wasn't. He seemed to rejoin me all at once.

He refreshed his coffee, grabbed his cup, pulled up a bar stool close, and sat down. Before he could even get used to the seat, he stood back up and started talking. Pacing and alternating between walking with his hands on his hips and using them to accentuate his point. The problem was that he was speaking so fast that I had no idea what he was talking about.

After a few minutes, he stopped and looked at me. He saw my expression and came back and took his seat again.

As if to reset, he did what he always does. He placed both elbows on the island with his hands palm to palm in a prayer position below his chin for a moment. Then he removed his glasses, ran one hand through his hair, and began to speak slower.

His words were less scattered and more deliberate the second time around. As if he had magically formed a plan in his mind over the course of the last few minutes.

"I will have to start from the beginning." He said.

He got up and retrieved a bottle of whiskey from behind a canister in his cabinet and poured a shot into his coffee. Without asking, he poured a dash into mine also.

Looking back, I am glad he did that.

"When I was born in 1951, my father was very young. He was 21, and my mother was 17. She died when I was three, and my father just didn't know how to raise a child by himself, or, if I am being completely honest with myself, he just didn't have an interest. As a result of that, my grandfather stepped in a lot to help out. I spent most of my time growing up with Grandpa, and he was more like my father than my actual father."

"Now, my grandfather Ed, by profession, was a mathematician. He was brilliant. He was, by all accounts, a genius. He had an uncanny ability to solve long algebraic equations in his head and found physics to be not just his passion but also a lifelong worthy cause. He was born in 1900, so he was able to consort with some of the world's greatest, including Einstein and Tesla, to name a couple. But, as you know, the closer a person is to genius, the more the line gets blurred into crazy. The two pretty much go hand in hand. He was no exception. He was eccentric, to say the least."

"He and my father were as opposite as night and day, and they never got along. But I found him fascinating and enjoyed him for who he was. He was philosophical, pragmatic, and reliable. He was the most beautiful realist. Even at an early age, I appreciated the fact that he seemed to know everything but never stopped looking."

"More than that, even though he saw every angle, he was a positive force. Always accepting of different outcomes, or seeing the good in people. He had a wonderful ability to see the redemptive qualities of any person or situation. It made him different. My childhood was great because of the interest he took in my life."

"Anyway, when I was nine years old, my father sent me away to boarding school in Brooklyn. I lived there for three years, and I'd never really left. Even my summer vacations were spent in the confines of the school walls."

"Until one holiday, my grandfather showed up. It was Christmas Eve 1963, and he somehow convinced the headmaster that he had permission to take me with him. After leaving, we went straight to the airport, and to my delight, ten hours later we landed in Cairo, Egypt. That trip sparked a love for Egypt in me that still remains today. But, more than that, it started a lifelong fascination with what I will explain to you now.   But I am getting ahead of myself."

He paused, filled both of our cups again with coffee and a larger dose of whiskey, then continued.

"My grandfather worked at Berkeley University in the math department. While there, he met and befriended a science history professor. To everyone's dismay, and despite the twenty-year age gap between the two, they became the best of friends. Spending all of their free time in each other's company, often leaving the country together. Two widowers, generations apart, with seemingly nothing in common."

"The professor told my grandfather a story. A story of a prince, five stones, and a cave that enabled time travel. Sound familiar?"

"It was the equivalent of an 'urban legend' in Egypt, as well as with all historians and archaeologists. A story that had been told and retold through the years but never really investigated until he began his own."

"I guess he told my grandfather in hopes of finding answers that he had given up on finding. He felt that if anyone could figure out the ins and outs of time travel, it would be my grandfather Ed. The professor spent most of his life tracking down clues and researching the subjects of the story. In fact, the portrait I showed you came from his personal belongings."

"At some point he took my grandfather to Egypt, and together, they searched for answers concerning the logistics of that possible portal described in the story."

"They did that for years, in secret. He never took

my grandfather to see it. He felt the more people knew, the stronger the possibility of someone else finding out."

"He and my grandfather both felt that if the word got out, the place would be taken apart or harmed in a way that if the time traveler was in the process of an experience, it would somehow trap him in the timeline he was currently in."

"Eventually, the professor died, and all his life's work, as well as his possessions and money, fell into the hands of my grandfather. Many of the notes you see on the table now are copies of the professor's journal."

"See? This is an entry from 1895."

He picked up the sheet and handed it to me. In immaculate cursive, it said,

December 2, 1895. 8/12 Slots filled. The last 4 Remaining.

Below it was a pencil sketch of a pyramid. At the top tip was what appeared to be a badly drawn hieroglyphic of a cat. The next row down was three circles. The row after that was four circles. Along the very bottom, from left to right, were four X's, followed by one circle.

I wasn't sure what to say. I just nodded and handed it back to him.

He continued.

"I don't think the old professor knew that my grandfather would become obsessed. Or maybe he did, and that's why he confided in him. At any rate, he did. From the day my grandfather got his hands on those notes, he became consumed with them. The rest of his life was devoted to the cause. At some point, he chose to turn down tenure at Berkeley so that he could relocate to Egypt and devote all of his time to it. Holidays and vacations were not enough. Like I said, he became obsessed."

No offense to Tom, but that came from a man who, in my eyes, did, in fact, appear obsessed.

Eight

We sat at that kitchen island for hours. The more he revealed, the more we drank.

It is as if he was trying to convince me when he had never been completely convinced himself.

Realization was washing over both of us at the same time. I believe alcohol made it easier to digest.

Tom got up, went into the kitchen and started making us a snack. (I think preparing food is another nervous habit of his.)

While he stood chopping up a salad, he continued explaining.

"It was on that trip to Egypt at thirteen that he sat me down and told me the complete tale. After moving to Egypt, he spent years studying the professor's notes and found the cave for himself. I was a skeptical kid, I suppose, because I didn't initially believe him. I probably never would have believed him had he not done what he did to convince me. It sounded like a made-up fairy tale to me."

"We were in Egypt about a week when he woke

me up late one night. He dressed me in warm clothing, and in complete darkness, we took a camel into the desert. I remember it so clearly."

"The moon gave the only light onto the dunes of the Sahara, and it seemed to me that we were aimlessly wandering. It took a few hours, and I had no idea where we were going. I don't remember feeling frightened, something I would recount later when I was older and took the trip on my own."

"As a child, I fell asleep on the back of that camel. Years later, as an adult, I was scared."

"The desert can play tricks on a person's mind at night. The sand appears to move. It is almost impossible to get and keep your bearings. He must have known that desert like the back of his hand, because without any issues, we went straight to the cave."

"However, I am not sure it should be called a cave. It would be more accurate to call it an underground room. It felt much like the burial chambers of the Pharaohs."

"That night I witnessed the wall for the first time myself. The pyramid was etched into a slab containing the stones, and it looked exactly like the professor's drawing."

"I didn't understand at the time that my grandfather wasn't just showing it to me, but he was checking the stones."

"On his first visit, the professor noted that there were five empty slots. On his notes for the second visit in 1895, there were four. I realize now that my grandfather was counting them. He was periodically going back to see if another slot was filled. Knowing that with each one, there was one less stone in the world to find. On our visit, there were three slots left."

"We didn't stay long. It was very important that we weren't seen going in or out, and so after about an hour, we started the long ride back. But it started a growing curiosity with me, one that still nags me today."

"That was the last time I saw my grandfather. My father was furious when he found out I wasn't at school. So, after my return, I wasn't allowed to see my grandfather again. A few years after that trip, he passed away."

"It was years later that I found out he left everything to me. His whole estate. Money, property, and all of the contents of his safe deposit box. These notes and maps were in that box. I found out at twenty-two that I had inherited it all. Which created an even greater rift between my father and me—one that was never repaired."

"The money he left me is how I was able to buy this house. The contents of that box and that trip to

Egypt with him have fueled a lifelong endeavor to do what I could to figure it out. I even changed my major in college because of it, which is how I met my wife."

We took a break from his story long enough to eat leftover pasta and salad. We were both buzzing at that point, and although I listened and heard every word he was saying, I hadn't accepted any of it yet.

After we ate, he cleared the dishes away. With new energy, he began to tell me more.

He left the room and came back holding what looked to be an overhead projector. After placing it on the kitchen counter and plugging it in, I realized it was an old portable microfiche machine. The kind used in libraries and newspaper rooms.

He reached into the manila folder and pulled out some old film, and as he sorted through it, he explained.

"This is where the story takes an interesting turn."

"I was working at the London Times. It was 1984, I believe, fairly early in my career. We had decided to run a story on the Holocaust. As more of an homage to the survivors than for awareness purposes. It was going to be a humanitarian piece, and I oversaw that project."

"We sent out feelers to get any photos previously

unseen to go with stories untold."

"You see, the Nazis had their hands in everything. If it made money or gave them strength, they went after it with veracity. That included priceless art and extended to anything they thought would improve their chances to outsmart the world. They wanted complete power."

"They caught wind of the story of the stones and spent years and substantial costs trying to prove or disprove the possibility of time travel."

"One day, the story of a survivor liberated from the Auschwitz concentration camp reached my desk. He told of a man captured by the Germans who was brought to the camp but segregated from the other prisoners. He was deemed a POW and had quarters away from the usually crowded dorms. The Jewish gentleman who came forward said that he had been in charge of taking care of the special captive. He was a doctor before the war, and so they gave him the task of keeping the man alive. Which would turn out to be quite difficult. "

"He said that the Germans cruelty to him was unlike any he had ever seen. They beat the man, starved him almost to death, and put him through hour after hour of questioning and torture. The odd part being that they were under strict instruction *not* to kill him. The Germans wanted something from him."

"Supposedly, when the man was captured and stripped, they discovered that he had a bar of gold in his possession. But not just any bar, a very specific bar. It was stamped with the crest of the Egyptian king from the story, along with a mint date of sometime in the 1600s. They were all but convinced he was the time-traveling prince, and so they held him captive, hoping one day pain and intimidation would cause him to break his silence."

"What made this particular man's story extra incredible was that he said shortly after this picture was taken, the man vanished. What I mean is, while these men and about thirty others were in a truck on the way to a local hospital set up to care for and house the victims of the concentration camps being liberated, the man evaporated. *Literally* vanished into thin air in front of a truck full of witnesses."

"Unfortunately, we couldn't find another man from the truck to verify his story in person. Most of them eventually died of old age, disease, or malnutrition, except for him. But we did find mention of it in two other handwritten accounts of that day. Accounts that were used to convict Germans of war crimes in the Nuremberg trials. All three of the men said exactly the same thing—he simply vanished into thin air."

Tom paused on a piece of microfiche. His glasses had slid down to the end of his nose. He looked over them at the fiche for a moment and then placed it into the machine. After viewing it, he moved aside.

He was grinning as he told me to.

"See for myself."

I wasn't sure what to expect. As I looked into the eye-piece, Tom said,

"This was taken on the day of liberation, January 27th, 1945."

It felt like college all over again; familiar. I'd spent hours doing the same thing for research those years. I focused on the picture in the viewfinder, and once I saw it, I couldn't physically move.

In front of me, removing any small bit of doubt that remained, was a picture of four men. All of them were dressed in stripes, with patches of hair over their skeletal heads, gaunt, and emaciated. Their eyes, though bulbous and fearful, were expressing relief or disbelief—I couldn't tell which.

They were all looking at the camera, except for one.

The man on the left—closest to the photographer—was looking to the right of the photo, dazed. It was a perfect profile picture. I immediately got emotional, and chills ran down my spine. My hair stood on end, and I had to pry myself away. I looked at Tom for a second, trying to come up with words—*any* words. But none would come.

My thoughts went to my phone and the picture I had taken of Alaa that day at the lake. I went and retrieved it.

As quickly as I could, I scrolled through my photos. When I found it, I handed it to Tom.

He stared at it for a moment, then covered his mouth and took two steps backwards and sat down. We both just looked at one another with the same reaction. We were both crying. Him from joy; me from every emotion under the sun.

I have never experienced anything quite like the feeling I had at that moment; I was overwhelmed.

I was ashamed. I was so disgusted with myself that I brushed off Alaa so carelessly when he tried to tell me. I felt horrible. But also, I felt relieved.

He wasn't mentally ill, and what he had gone through was horrifying; sympathy enveloped me as though it were coursing through my veins. But, more than any of it, I felt *love*.

It's sad to say that I needed the indisputable proof in front of me before I could allow myself to admit and feel the real and complete love I had for him. That was a life-defining moment.

What followed all of those emotions—once it sank in—were questions. So many questions started running through my mind all at once, at lightning speed. I had so much to ask him. So much to find out.

And so many apologies to make.

When we had both absorbed it as much as we were able, and I regained control of my mind once more, I took my phone from Tom. I scrolled through my photos once again and found the picture I had snapped of the stone.

I don't think I've ever seen anyone filled with as much joy as he was at that time. His smile couldn't have been bigger.

His eyes were filled with tears as he said,

"The only time I have seen this stone was beside the others in the wall of that cave. There is absolutely no doubt that this is an exact replica of them. The story is real. This can't be happening."

We both just sat lost in our own thoughts for a moment. Silent in our disbelief. Or more accurately, our final and complete belief.

"Cate, I have so many questions. If he could return, what kept him at the concentration camp? Why didn't he just leave before it got bad? Why did he wait for liberation and suffer those years?"

Tom kept staring at my phone as he spoke.

"The last time I made that trip was twelve years ago, and the second spot from the end was filled. There were only two slots left. One spot on either side. If the order has been top to bottom, right to left, as Arabic is normally read, that means one spot was skipped. A fact that has been the cause of many sleepless nights for me."

"I finally gave up after that, feeling I would never figure this all out before they were all used. Cate, if you only saw one stone—I mean, if Alaa only has one—where is the other one, and why did he change the order?"

"I don't know, Tom. I don't even know where he is to ask him. I believe I have hurt him to the point that even if I did know, he wouldn't trust me enough to tell me. Truthfully, I can't blame him. Hell, I wouldn't blame him if he never spoke to me again."

"Oh my God, Tom, what if he has gone?"

Any buzz I had from the alcohol was quickly gone, and I needed a drink. Foregoing the coffee nips we had enjoyed until then, I got the bottle and filled two glasses; I emptied half my glass in one gulp.

When my mind slowed enough to regain my senses, I asked Tom what he thought I should do. At that point, being convinced seemed worse than not believing. I had the feeling I had damaged us beyond repair.

"Listen, Cate. If all of this is true—and it obviously is—then if there is anything we should take away from it, it is to believe in fate. Omitting the time travel and everything that goes along with that mind-scramble, you have to believe that you two are destined to be together. In this life or another, right?"

I downed the rest of my whiskey and stared at the table in front of me.

"Oh, Tom, how could I be so careless? Why didn't I just shut up and listen to him when I had the chance?"

"Kiddo, don't be so hard on yourself. No one—and I do mean *no one*—in your shoes would have believed his story. Again, is it just an accident that you even know me and I have a connection to all of this? Or is this the way it was supposed to play out?"

"All that matters is that you know *now*. What you do with this information is up to you."

He grabbed my hand across the table and held it.

"Cate, there is one more thing I want you to know."

Oh, *good grief.* I wasn't sure I could take any more, but I prepared myself just the same.

He downed his glass in one swallow before continuing.

"I wasn't completely honest about my wife Caroline. She and I met in college just before I found out about my inheritance. Even before I had money, she agreed to marry me. Both of us were passionate about our work in Egypt and spent all of our summers helping excavate various sites. We donated our time to learn because we enjoyed it so much. It was all so very unglamorous, but we relished the time spent together. We felt like we were making a difference in our way."

"In our second year of marriage, our third year of university, she was diagnosed with breast cancer."

"The doctors were unclear at first, and even though many tests had confirmed the diagnosis, they were not finished with her evaluation. They needed more tests to come up with a definitive diagnosis and treatment plan—tests they had administered shortly before our summer trip to Egypt that year."

"Caroline watched her own mother die of breast cancer. It was a slow, horrible three years before she finally passed, and Caroline witnessed her battle from the beginning to the end. She was terrified of the process."

"She didn't want to wait around until she became emaciated and dependent on me. The treatment actually scared her more than dying. She wanted to die on her own terms."

"Caroline didn't die from cancer; she committed suicide."

"One night, like many other nights before, we were due at an excavation site. That time she opted to remain behind and claimed that she was tired. I kissed her goodbye, and when I returned the next morning, she was hanging by a bedsheet from our sixth-floor balcony."

"It was the first thing I saw when I turned down the path to our apartment. I do not know how long she'd been there or why no one else saw her before I did. If anyone would have looked up, they would have seen her. I haven't been able to rid myself of that fact for almost fifty years."

"The tragedy being that she was misdiagnosed."

"When I returned home to America, there was a message on our machine to call the doctor's office, more specifically the pathologist. When I did, they informed me that she did *not* have cancer; she had Paget's disease. An illness that mimics cancer in a lot of ways."

"Had cell phones been a thing back then, we would have gotten the news sooner, and it all would have turned out differently. She killed herself over a disease she didn't even have, and it will haunt me always."

"It is one of the reasons I kept searching for the answers to the stones. If she would have known what I knew just five days later, she would be alive today. Paget's disease of the bone is usually fatal, but Paget's of the breast is completely treatable."

"If I could have found the stones, discovered the

secrets, and gone back, maybe she would have lived a full life."

"If that is even how they work—now I'm not so sure. It appears your prince has been time-jumping to the future. I don't know anymore. So many *unknowns* and *maybes*."

"What I regret the most is that I wasn't able to give her the life and love that she deserved. Maybe I would have failed her no matter what, but the thought of having the chance to find out kept me searching much longer than I should have. And, to make matters worse, I never told her I knew where the cave was. I did as the professor and my grandfather had done and remained the only person who knew. I only told her half of the story. I don't know why I did that. I allowed her to take second place behind my work and never even told her what she was *taking a seat behind*. That is guilt I've had to live with."

"Cate, don't make the same mistake I did. With or without proof of all of this, you *knew* you loved him. I saw it in your eyes when you told me about him and your time together. Hell, I saw it on your face long before you opened up and told me at all. I haven't learned much in this life—not what others would consider valuable information to pass on or to help mankind—but the one thing I have learned from loss and ignorance is that love is worth taking the risk. It doesn't come around often, and most people go their whole lives without it."

"Even though you have strange circumstances surrounding this connection, it is indeed love—on a soul level. And the fact is that *you are* the girl in the story. He traveled from two hundred years ago to be with you, and that is extraordinary. No matter what, this is now an undeniable fact."

When he was finished, my tears were free flowing. I knew he was right, and all I could think about was going to find Alaa.

130

Nine

It was Sunday, and I woke up with a hangover. Something I hadn't done since college. Suddenly I knew why I had stopped that behavior; I felt terrible.

I made my way to the kitchen in a fog. Coffee was made, and I grabbed a cup. I avoided looking in the direction of all of the papers scattered out onto the island from the night before. I wasn't ready to start again. I needed aspirin and caffeine.

I made myself a piece of toast and sat down at the dining room table.

Facts from the night before were gradually making their way back into my half-awake brain. Again, I had to convince myself, with all of the proof revealed to me just hours before, that it was actually *real*. I had all of the evidence I needed, but logically, it still seemed so far-fetched.

I walked over to the island and picked up one of the sheets. It was a map of some sort. The next one that caught my eye was labeled "Laila." I scanned the page.

It was a list of dates and personal information, such as her place of birth and family history. There were many pages just like that one, each with a different subject listed at the top.

Most were journal pages with specific entry dates. Each visit to the cave was documented. Between Tom, the professor, and his grandfather, there were hundreds of them. Some listed three or four visits in the same year, and then there were years skipped. He had them in chronological order.

I put them back exactly where I got them and went out to the porch.

I remember having a nagging feeling that something was missing. I wasn't sure what it was until I realized Sheba wasn't pestering me for her morning meal. I thought back to the night before and remembered the last time I'd seen her. It was when we were together on the couch.

I spent the next hour searching for her. Yelling,

"Here, kitty, kitty!" and rattling a bag of food. She was nowhere to be found, inside or out.

Tom came in from the stables and removed his heavy coat.

"How do you feel this morning, kiddo?"

I wasn't sure how to answer that. Physically, I felt awful; mentally and emotionally, I was in limbo. He got a cup of coffee and took a seat next to me at the dining table. I watched him pack his pipe with tobacco.

He seemed like a different person to me than he had been just twenty-four hours before. I guess previously I hadn't really known him. Discovering what makes a person tick—or their passions—changes the way we view them. He had become a father figure to me overnight. Something I had never had before.

There was so much depth to him. For four years, I had only viewed him as a hard-nosed boss and workaholic.

"I feel like I've been hit in the head with a hammer, to be honest. Have you seen Sheba?"

"I can't say that I have; I'm sure she will turn up. Probably chasing mice in the barn. She'll come around when she's hungry."

I spent that day much like I had the days of the week before. Tending his garden, cooking, and just trying to get through it. With one major difference, my new knowledge made it impossible for me to relax or think about anything else.

I went over the story a million times. Each time, I generated more questions.

A Prince. I had fallen in love with a time-traveling prince. Better than any story I could have ever made up. Actually, I *couldn't* have made it up.

Would anything ever make sense? My whole life, all I ever hoped and strived for was a normal life. And although I wasn't ever sure what a normal life included, I knew it did not include any of what was in mine then.

By late afternoon, I felt like a ticking time bomb. I tried to read a book or help Tom in the kitchen, but whatever I attempted to do, I failed.

We sat down to eat, and I picked at my food. I couldn't take it anymore. Finally, I said out loud what I had been thinking all day.

"Tom, I think I need to go try and find him."

Tom put his fork down, smiled and said,

"Cate, what in the hell are you waiting for? It took you long enough. Get your things; I'll drive you to the train station."

I packed up, and after one final unsuccessful search for Sheba, we headed out.

The drive was a quiet one, even though I know he had just as many questions as I did.

I think we both knew discussing them wouldn't bring any more understanding than we already had. The realization was that if I couldn't find Alaa, they would be unanswered for the rest of our lives. Neither one of us wanted to consider that. So, we stayed silent. Both of us put faith in the *"powers that be"* that I would find him.

It was cold and drizzling when we arrived at the station. I'll say again, so much of my time since coming to this country has been spent wet. I grabbed my backpack out of the truck, and Tom walked me in to buy my ticket. We were standing on the platform, he with his hands in his front pockets, teetering back and forth from his heels to his toes, and me, unsure of what to say.

As my train pulled in, he retrieved an envelope from his back pocket and held it out to me. I took it from him, and when I peeled back the flap and peered inside, I saw that it was a stack of cash. I rejected it and tried to hand it back, but he only pushed it back at me.

"Look, you have a long road ahead of you. Neither of us is really sure where it is going to take you. I have spent my whole life accumulating money that I didn't need, with nothing I ever really wanted to spend it on. Accept this from me, Cate. I don't have children, but if I did, I would want to help them in any way that I could. Let me give you this gift. Don't deny an old man the happiness of being a part of something so grand and beautiful. In a way, you are living my dream. Please let me feel like I'm a part of the outcome, even if only in the smallest of ways. Besides, if it weren't for you, I never would have known the truth."

In the end, I couldn't refuse him, and with a

constricted throat, I thanked him.

"And don't worry, I'll call you when Sheba shows up. I'll take care of her. Go find him, and call me if you need anything. Keep me in the loop. Okay?"

"I will."

He waited on the platform in the rain until my train pulled away, waving goodbye.

When he was out of sight, I sat back in my chair and tried to form a plan. Which was much harder than you could imagine. I was in uncharted territory. The only examples I had to base my beliefs on were Hollywood cinematic depictions of how things worked. Romantic time travel movies. None of them ever explained anything I could use in my *very real* scenario. They weren't real; what I faced was.

When I got to London, I still didn't have a realistic plan.

Tired and frustrated, I hopped on the only bus line running to my area that night, the 220.

I was staring out the window, thinking about Sheba. I was in my own little bubble. I was not really paying attention to anything around me until someone caught my eye.

A few rows up, standing in the disabled section, was an older gentleman in a long trench coat, and he was staring at me. Silver hair, a full gray beard, and some silent, unknown quality that demanded my focus. He looked haggard, his eyes hooded with bushy gray eyebrows and a serious glare I couldn't look away from. I watched him for a few minutes; he seemed out of place.

When he got off of the bus at the next stop, I observed him stepping down. Once he was a few feet away on the sidewalk, I saw that there was a little dog at his side. A little white dog. A dog that looked a lot like Mishmish.

By the time the possibility of what I might have been looking at registered, it was too late.

I hesitated too long, and the bus took off again. I jumped up, pushed the button, and after a few minutes of persistent begging, persuaded the driver to stop.

I ran out the door as quickly as I could and rushed back to the previous stop. We had only gone three blocks, but he wasn't there. I searched and searched. I went down the street, across the street, and even into a few alleyways; still, no sign of him.

After exhausting all efforts—and feeling as if I were losing my mind—I walked in the rain the nine blocks home.

***

That week was difficult, to say the least.

I woke up one day with what felt like the flu. It seemed like every time I turned around; I was sick. I took over-the-counter cold medicine and refused to stay down. I had too much to do, and I couldn't rest anyway. It seemed as though I was rushing against an imaginary deadline.

Real or not, it kept me moving forward.

I called Alaa so many times in those days, I lost count. I left repeated messages for him to call me and never got a response. I realized that if I was going to have a chance in hell of finding him, I was going to have to put in the work.

I started with the easiest location first. I remembered the hotel we spent the night in and how familiar he had been with the guy at the front desk. He treated it as if it were a home away from home. If he needed time away from his shared apartment to be alone, that would be the closest possible place for him to go. It had everything he would need to live and regroup and was still close enough to the hospital to get to work when he needed to.

But when I arrived, the person manning the front desk was not the same. And, to make matters worse, he seemed to struggle with English. I tried to explain what I needed, and he was perplexed. He had no idea who Alaa was, and I had my doubts that he understood what I was saying at all. I took a seat and waited for his shift to end so that I could talk to the next person on duty.

Around noon, the man I was familiar with showed up. His nametag said "Omar," and I was overjoyed, but it was short-lived. Even though he knew who I was asking about, he hadn't seen him since the night we were there together. I left feeling defeated.

I walked the same path we had taken to the train that night. I tried to come up with some kind of plan, but it seemed all I could think about was that last night Alaa and I spent together. Memories flooded my mind and rendered me useless. I felt so much remorse and regret. I thought of the way he had owned me that night, before he told me the story.

It brought me comfort on some level, but it also put me in a place I had never been. I felt grief. Missing another human to that extent was an emotion I wasn't familiar with, and *it hurt*.

I walked a while and hadn't been paying attention until I looked up and realized where I was.

In front of me was the shop where Alaa and I had stopped for coffee. I looked over to the bench.

On it were two people. She with her fur-lined coat and hat, and he with his beanie and scarf. He had his hand on her thigh, leaning into her, and they were both laughing. I just stood there; I couldn't look away. Until the man of the twosome raised his head.

Jesus, it was Michael.

I collected myself and kept walking as fast as I could. I half walked, half jogged until I got to the underground and slowed down. After the first flight of stairs, I paused long enough to look back, and to my relief, there was no one behind me. Thank God he hadn't followed. Maybe he hadn't seen me?

Still shaken, I boarded the train.

Michael was a part of my past that I had no desire to revisit. I quickly dismissed the incident and got back to the task at hand.

After calming down and reevaluating, I decided pretty quickly that the next logical thing for me to do was pay a visit to Alaa's job.

I got some rest, and the next morning I found myself in the surgery consultation department of the Royal London hospital. Looking back, I probably should have planned better.

I came out of the elevator and was face-to-face with the receptionist before I'd even considered what I would say. After telling her who I was looking for, she shut me down almost immediately.

The girl was young and cute. I could tell by the expression on her face that she knew exactly who I was talking about the second I mentioned him. I've seen that spark in a girl's eyes too many times.

After arguing and getting nowhere with her, I

changed my tactic to being polite and explained to her that it was a family emergency. She still wouldn't budge.

I had all but given up and got into the elevator to leave. Just as the doors started closing, someone yelled for me to hold them open.

A man got in and introduced himself.

"I'm Kevin. I didn't mean to eavesdrop, but I heard you asking about Dr. Attia."

"Yeah, do you know when he will be in?"

The guy was young, donned scrubs, and was full of nervous energy. Chewing gum and wearing earbuds. He seemed to be yelling over his own music still playing in his ears. But—then again—he was American. One thing I have noticed since living abroad is that they all have issues with volume control.

"Wait, sorry." He said.

He got his phone from his pocket and turned the music off, and when he spoke again, it was at a normal volume. Thank God for small favors; my head was already killing me.

"I am one of Alaa's flatmates. Listen, we have all kind of been worried about him. All I can tell you is that he requested some personal time off a few weeks ago, took his dog, and hasn't been back. He didn't move out of his room but took most everything with him. Which is odd, because he literally never takes time off. Well, more than a week at a time anyway."

"Shit. Do you remember exactly when that was?"

"I could get into a world of trouble for telling you any of this, you know, privacy policy and all. But I suppose it's okay since you said it was a family emergency."

He paused, put his index finger up, and tapped his lip—as if trying to think. I saw an understanding form in his mind. The proverbial light bulb went on. He retrieved his phone again and scrolled through his messages.

"Yes, it was November 26th. He messaged me to let me know he had left his mailbox key in our shared kitchen and asked me to collect it while he was gone."

The elevator stopped, and we both got out. I thanked him. He was walking backwards away from me, as he said,

"I wish I knew more. The guy is pretty private concerning his personal life. I hope this helped!"

He turned around, put his hand up as a quick goodbye, and left.

Though I was glad to have the information, I wasn't sure what to do with it.

I made my way to the underground and tried to

think of what to do next. It was still early enough in the day that going to Scotland was possible.

I considered it, but I wondered if I could manage to find the cottage on my own. I searched my map timeline on my phone to see if the location had been saved, and it had. I was still a little doubtful.

All I knew was that I couldn't give up; I had to try everything. Maybe he just went for a bit of rest and reset? Any thought was better than the one where he ditched 2019 altogether and I would never see him again. My mind was made up before I even got out of the tube.

Ten

I arrived in Edinburgh just after midnight. I found a cab, showed him the location, and after a few minutes we were headed to the cottage. It turned out to be only ten miles away from the airport.

It was obvious from the second we arrived that Alaa was not there. There was no car, no lights, and no signs of life. I felt immediate, overwhelming sadness and just sat in the cab, trying to come to terms with the fact it was a wasted trip. Until the driver spoke and snapped me back into the real world.

It was—without a doubt—the strongest Scottish accent I had ever heard. It took me a second to understand what he was saying.

"Madam, thirty-seven pounds."

I apologized and started fumbling for my wallet. I hadn't stopped for cash, and after a temporary panic, I remembered the money Tom had given me. I sorted through my bag and found it.

As I pulled out the money to pay him, a smaller

envelope fell out. I tucked the envelope and its unknown contents into my coat pocket, grabbed my backpack, and then walked the short distance to the door.

There was no moon that night, and after the cab pulled away, it was pitch dark.

I stood in front of that cottage door, just staring at it. I am not sure why. I guess I was scared. Frightened that I would go in and find everything gone, or maybe I was scared of what I was about to experience returning to the place that was a physical reminder of Alaa himself. Or maybe it was a sad reminder and solid proof of his absence. Whatever it was, I was frozen in place. I stood there watching the fog from my own breath, delaying the inevitable.

After summoning all of my courage, I tried the door, and it was locked. I grabbed a chair from the porch and stood on it to reach above the door frame, but after a few attempts, I still couldn't find it. I was tired, my back and feet were aching something terrible, and it looked like I was going to be sleeping on the porch.

There was an empty ceramic plant holder near the steps. I grabbed it and placed it upside-down on top of the chair so that I could reach farther. Using my cellphone for a flashlight, I finally found the key, and shortly after, I was in.

I stood just inside the doorway and let my eyes

adjust. Even after turning on the lamp, I didn't move from the entryway. Taking extra time to scan the room and take in my surroundings.

It looked exactly how it had the day we left. Nothing out of place. Except that the books that were once scattered about the room had all been returned to their places on the shelves. Something about that saddened me.

It was colder inside than it was out.

I immediately headed to the fireplace to build a fire. Fresh wood was already stacked in the grate. All I had to do was put some tinder in and light it. Within a few minutes, I had it going. I lay on the sofa, in my coat, watching the flames.

As the heat gradually started to fill the room, I removed my shoes and, still fully clothed, curled up. The next thing I remember was waking up to frigid air and morning light coming in the window.

I got up, rebuilt the fire, and put on the kettle. All I could find was a canister of Turkish coffee and tea. Since I didn't know how to make the coffee, I had to settle for the latter.

I ached all over and felt feverish, and I could no longer ignore the fact that I was sick. I took my tea and sat on the hearth. I couldn't even consider what I should do when all I could think of was sleep.

I willed myself away from the fire, made a bath,

and climbed in it.

As I lay there, finally feeling warm for the first time in days, I couldn't help but give into my emotions. I allowed myself to feel what I had avoided for weeks. Tears were flowing, and I let them. Completely and utterly. My head was stopped up, I had a fever, my legs and ankles were swollen twice their size, and my back ached.

I had rejected and pushed away the only man I had ever loved, and I was out of answers. I honestly did not know what to do. And so I just remained in the bath and had a complete meltdown.

Afterwards, I went into the armoire to get the robe that he had so graciously left out for me when we were there together. Hanging beside it was the green evening dress. I lingered there, touching the satin fabric for a moment. Memories and emotions making my heart feel as if it would explode. When had I become such a weak person? I put the robe on and left the room sobbing—again.

I took two more cold tablets and sat in front of the fire to brush out my hair. After making myself another cup of tea and eating some soup that was in the cabinet, I grabbed the copy of Jane Eyre from the shelf and tried to relieve myself of my own thoughts. The only way I knew to self-soothe. It wasn't long before I was asleep.

I spent three days in the cottage. Eating soup,

drinking tea, and feeling forlorn. Physically, I knew I couldn't continue my search for him until I was healthy enough to do so, and being in his cottage made me feel better.

I enjoyed lying on his couch, seeing his jacket hanging on the hall tree, and the comfort of his familiar scent.

I think that is what got me through those days. Just being in his space, surrounded by his things— things that he loved. It made me feel close to him, and it was all I had. I lived each day with the hope that he would walk through the door any second.

Eventually I ran out of wood and had to go find the woodpile outside. It was stacked by a shed behind the cottage. It took every ounce of my strength to bring in bundles, but it was either that or freeze to death.

After a few trips, curiosity got the better of me, and I decided to investigate the shed. The door was not locked, but there was a log on the ground blocking the door. It took multiple tries to roll the log out of the way, but I managed to move it just enough that I could squeeze my body through.

Once inside, I used my cell phone flashlight and looked around.

Hanging on the walls were old tools and farm equipment, rusted and covered in cobwebs. Nothing out of the ordinary.

There were a few boxes labeled *"medical textbooks."* I pulled back the top of one and saw that was exactly what was in them. It looked as if nothing in the room had been touched for years.

In the corner was an old ammo box, the kind with lids that have to be nailed down. But what was different about it was that it was the only thing in the room that was *not* covered in dust and spiderwebs. I set my phone down and tried to remove the cover. It was, in fact, nailed down.

I scanned the walls for something I could use as leverage and found an old saw. Not my first choice, but I didn't see another option. I slid it under the edge and tried to lift the lid. It wouldn't budge. I went in the house and grabbed a butter knife, and finally, I was able to pry it up.

Inside, covered with a wool blanket, were two smaller boxes. One was a portable file box. I opened it first.

I removed the bag inside and sat down on the dirt floor to empty its contents. It was a cardboard tube. After popping off the end, I pulled a small stack of papers out. Even with the light from my phone, I couldn't make out what they said. I decided to take it into the house and turned my attention to the other box.

It contained a leather bag. When I tried to lift the bag out of the box, it was really heavy. I untied the drawstring and shined light into the bag. I heard myself say,

"Holy shit!"

Not just once, but I said it a few times. It contained three gold bars.

After the shock wore off, I wrapped them up, put them back, and went into the house with the cardboard tube under my arm.

I sat down at the desk and spread the papers out. There were five sheets in all. Most contained names listed from top to bottom. The first sheet was a list of German names; the second and third were what appeared to be Jewish. The last two sheets were written in German; the only things I could read and understand were names and dates. The one across the top said EVELINA MEYER, 1920-1945.

I took a picture of each page so that I could email them to Tom. Then I placed them in the tube and put them back where I had gotten them.

That night I had trouble sleeping. I knew what I needed to do, but for those days I just couldn't bring myself to do it.

Finally, on the last day, I couldn't put it off any longer. I had avoided the box on the mantle since my arrival. I knew that it contained the answer to the most pressing question of all, but I just kept putting it off. It was some kind of stupid effort to delay—or deny—the truth.

I was shaking when I went to the drawer to get the key.

I moved the leather folder aside in search of it, but it wasn't there. I methodically checked all of the drawers in succession, with each failure creating more panic. By the time I got to the last one, my heart was pounding. It wasn't there.

I went over to the mantle and—without a key—lifted the lid of the box and peered inside.

It was empty. The box was empty. No stone, no rings. It didn't initially register.

I picked up the box and spotted the key lying under it. I carried it to the couch and sat there with the empty box in my lap, trying to understand the implications. My head wouldn't accept what the empty box surely meant.

Distraught, I put on my coat and went out onto the porch. I had to get out of that room.

I sat outside, in the freezing cold, with so much pain in my heart I felt physically sick to my stomach. I was so shocked; I couldn't even cry.

In a daze, I put my hands in my pockets and, without intention, pulled out the envelope that I had placed there three days before. Not really thinking,

I opened it.

Inside were two sheets of paper. The first was a note from Tom:

Cate,

Four years after Caroline died, in 1979, I made one of my yearly treks to the cave. On that visit, although there were no new slots taken, I did discover a bag left on the ground in front of the wall of stones. Inside was a letter, as well as a bar of gold. I am not sure why either was left behind; they are the only things that have ever been found there.

A copy of the letter is enclosed. The original, as well as the gold, is in a safe place for now. This has remained the biggest mystery to date. I've also included the microfiche surrounding the 1945 incident, in case you need it for anything.

I don't know if it will help, but maybe it would mean something to Alaa when you find him.

Happy hunting,

~Tom

The second sheet of paper was a photocopy of an old sheet, tattered on the edges, and written in beautiful script. As I began to read it, I realized it was familiar. I knew the words.

I jumped up, went into the house, and searched the leather folder until I found the page I was looking for. I placed them side by side, and they were almost identical. The only difference was the handwriting style and the way Lysette was signed at the bottom. One was written in cursive, while the other was written in block letters.

I sat there rereading them, over and over. Trying to make sense of it. It was something I realized pretty quickly I was not going to understand. Alaa was the only one that would be able to shed light on it.

I went to my backpack and got my notebook. The one I usually use for work facts and journalism work.

I recorded all of the dates and details surrounding every single encounter with Alaa since I met him. Everything he told me and all that Tom had. It seemed so very important to me all of a sudden. It took hours, and when I was finished, I felt renewed. So much so that I tore out a sheet and wrote what was in my heart. The first time I had had the inclination to write in months.

The fact was that Alaa was gone, and in all probability, I would never see him again. At least, not in this lifetime. That fact created the need in me to write, and so I did...

 *The morning was cool and drizzly, but it was not quite raining.*

Neither of us was fully awake to the day.

And both were still digesting what had transpired the night before.

We ran across the busy London Street, trying to beat the traffic light and grabbed our coffee and raisin pastries on the go.

Under an ominous sky,

We sat down on a bench outside of the shop for an impromptu brunch.

We were at an odd crossroads.

Happy in our togetherness, but equally confused as to where to go from there.

We slipped back into friendship mode so very easily.

Sitting there, smiling, drinking our coffee, and teasing each other.

Laughing, prolonging our time together,

Unsure of when we would meet again.

Pigeons gathered just out of reach to snatch up the crumbs.

We only had a few hours before we would go our separate ways.

As it started to rain,

You opened up my pink umbrella and held it over my head while I finished eating.

Do you remember the comment you made about my choice of the color pink?

I do, and it makes me smile, even now.

I unexpectedly came upon that bench the other day.

As I observed another couple sitting there,

Dangerously close to one another,

Sipping their coffee and chatting,

I was flooded with all of the thoughts and feelings I had tried in vain to ignore.

It felt strange.

As if somehow that space was reserved only for us, until I saw them occupying it.

I had to stand there until it sank in. To give my grief space to be felt.

Whether it was out of respect for you or so that I could embrace the memory fully and completely, I do not know.

I just stood there and let it wash over me.

The sadness, the loss, the tinge of jealousy over what we had once shared.

It seems like a million years, but it was not so long ago.

This continues to be one of my favorite memories of

us.

The way we interacted with each other, the simple joy and safety of it.

I couldn't have been happier than I was that day.

Sitting under a pink umbrella with you in the London rain.

I felt like I belonged and didn't wish to be anywhere else.

A part of me will always yearn for that version of us.

That version of me.

The version that only you and those particular circumstances of that day could bring out.

It was magic.

Memories are a gift.

A beautiful way that we can enjoy someone after they are no longer a part of our lives.

I realize now that I don't ever want to forget that day.

Or any of the days leading up to it.

I will instead hold close every detail.

And put them where they belong.

*~**Cate***

I placed it into the leather folder with the rest of them, tied it up, and placed it back into the drawer.

I was *not* okay. But I knew one way or another I would be. And so, I cleaned up the cottage, packed my bag, and called an Uber. I was going home.

Eleven 

I started to give up. Not willingly, but more because I had run out of ideas and was trying to be realistic. By all appearances and from the clues I had managed to gather, he was gone. I had to resign myself to the facts and accept them.

I tried to adopt the view that if our lives were entangled because of fate, whatever was meant to be would be, and I shifted my focus to giving up any control I imagined I had.

I said *"imagined"* because I truly feel now that having control is all in my head. My future—our destiny—was never really in my control to begin with. But I wasn't completely convinced of that at the time.

And if I tell you now that I believed I had accomplished all that I could and gotten from our story all that I would get and wrapped it up into a neat little package and put it behind me, well then, there wouldn't be much more to write.

There wouldn't be a story. And since you are

reading this now, obviously that is not the case.

There was more. The same way the universe lined things up for me to meet Alaa and start our journey in this life, it did again. Making it possible for me to keep following the breadcrumbs until I got some answers.

A few days after being home, I went out for supplies. On top of battling a bit of depression and missing Sheba, I still wasn't feeling my best. I made an appointment with my doctor for the following day and decided to take it easy and stay in that evening.

Arms full of groceries I opened my apartment door, and there, sitting on my couch, was Michael.

He was stretched out, one foot on my coffee table, not even looking guilty or bothered that he had let himself in—or that I had caught him. On the contrary, he appeared to be waiting on me.

After the initial shock wore off, the only thing I could think to say was,

"What in the hell are you doing here?"

He didn't budge from his place and actually looked annoyed at my reaction. Like I had interrupted him. He always had such a disposition of entitlement. Annoyingly so. That day was no different.

"Glad to see you too, Catie. How was your trip?" Was his reply—and he still didn't move from my couch.

He was sitting there with something in his hand—my notebook—along with all of my personal pages surrounding him. It infuriated me. I ran over and began collecting them, starting with the page in his hand. It was the letter from Tom.

"What in the fuck is wrong with you? What gives you the right to go through my stuff?"

He sat up lazily, as if to accentuate the point that he was unfazed. An act that was taken for exactly what it was: intimidation. It was his way. A practice that had gotten him far in his life. Experience had perfected it, and I almost felt like I should be the one defending myself for some crime instead of him. He said,

"I knew that guy wasn't going to go away."

I was putting my papers back into my notebook. At first, what he said didn't register. But then, it did.

"What do you mean? what guy?"

He rolled his eyes, then got up and followed me across the room. I put the notebook on my table and started putting my groceries away. He leaned on the kitchen doorframe.

"Oh, come on, Catie, you don't actually believe this shit, do you? That man obviously has a screw loose. Literally anyone could hear Tom's theories and become the person in that story."

I paused; something didn't make sense. He wasn't shocked; he acted as if all of the information he just read was old news.

"How do you know about *any of this*, Michael?"

He smiled, seeming pretty proud of himself for getting my attention.

"Catie, my uncle kept those files in his work desk at the paper for years. Of course I read them. Hell, he was the laughingstock of my family the whole time I was growing up. We all knew he was obsessed. It was a running family joke. We all knew he took after our crazy grandfather."

He looked amused, and for a fleeting second, I was filled with doubt and felt foolish. He continued.

"I knew that guy would show back up. I knew he was some kind of conman years ago."

"Michael, *WHAT MAN?*"

"This Alaa guy." He passed by me to grab a bottle of water from my fridge.

"How do you know him? You are not making any sense."

He took his water, sat down at my table, and lit a cigarette, knowing I didn't allow smoking in my house. I was too invested in his reply to complain. I grabbed a saucer for him to use as an ashtray.

"Well?" I said.

He hesitated, choosing his words carefully for once. He narrowed his eyes, and I could tell he was studying any reaction I might have as he said them.

"He came to the paper three years ago and asked for me. When I invited him into my office, he said he was there to drop off a cash gift for one of my journalists. He specifically asked that the money be used for your student loans. He wanted all of your debt to be paid off. Anonymously."

I stood in my kitchen for a moment, trying to accept the new information before I reacted.

"So, let me get this straight. You didn't pay off my debt, but you took credit for it."

He was staring at me, smiling. My God, he was handsome. I was never as sure of that fact than I was at that moment—because there were no feelings involved. There was no emotional or mental involvement anymore. And he was still drop-dead gorgeous. Tall, chiseled physique, blond-headed, and blue-eyed. He looked like a Greek God, and it never mattered less to me than it did to me then.

He was attempting to win me over with his boyish charm. But I was long since immune to that tactic, and I was genuinely pissed off.

"Look, he wanted it done anonymously; it was just easier to let you assume I did it. I saw no harm in it. Still don't."

Of course he didn't. That man had never had any morals or integrity. He used it as manipulation. My mind was racing. I stayed in our miserable relationship long after it was over because I felt as if I owed him. I saw good in him that wasn't ever there. I was livid.

"Come on, Catie! He's a common criminal! He said he wanted to leave the gift as a birthday present and wouldn't say how he knew you. I figured he had seen your recent article and had formed some kind of odd obsessive crush. I was protecting you, and it appears I was correct to do so. I always knew you were gullible, but this is ridiculous."

I tried to stay calm. But one main thing kept going through my mind.

"Michael, when did he come to the office? Do you remember?"

He put out his cigarette and answered as he was blowing out the last of the smoke.

"Yeah, I do. Only because it was December 19th, and he had missed your birthday by a week."

I tried not to appear anything other than annoyed, but my stomach was in knots and my heart must have been beating a mile a minute. He knew of me three years ago. *Three years.*

Why did he wait? My mind went immediately to the bus incident. Was that chance, or had he planned that first meeting? Everything I thought I knew came into question. I needed to be alone.

"Michael, you need to go."

He stood, walked to me, and put his hand up against my cheek.

"I've missed you, Catie. I was upset when you didn't stop and say hello the other day. I saw you, and I *know* you noticed me."

Oh God, I hated it when he called me that. I shuddered at his touch.

"Michael, Agnes is on her way over. So unless you want everyone in the office to know you were here, you need to go."

His disposition changed, and he pulled his hand back, as if I were fire. He looked angry and spoke through gritted teeth.

"Now you listen to me, Catie. I don't know what your connection is with this guy, but if he is who he says he is, I will find out. I will find the stones, and I will do what I need to do to gain access to this. There is no record of that man before eleven years ago. No birth records, no family, and no information. As if he didn't exist before then. If you do not help me, then at the very least, I will be the one to break the story. He will be exposed as a fraud, lose his medical license, and his life will end as he knows it. Do you understand what I am saying? If I am not included in this, I will make his life so miserable and difficult that he will never be able to return to wherever it is he is from."

After pulling away, he straightened up and zipped his jacket, winked at me, and said,

"Think about it."

And then he casually walked out of my door.

I was physically repulsed and shivered.

I followed him to the door and locked the deadbolt. I sat down at my dining room table, trying to process all that Michael had said. What had me so upside-down was the date on which Alaa had gone to the office.

When I was a young girl, there was a discrepancy in the date of my birth. The copy of my birth certificate from the office of vital statistics said December 12th. But the written copy from the hospital said the 19th. My whole life I had gone by the first date, always knowing that my real birthday was the latter. I told no one.

I picked up my phone and called Tom. He answered on the second ring.

"Hey Cate, how goes it?"

Listen. Tom, I just got a visit from Michael; I'll explain all of that later. But is there anything in your notes or paperwork that says when Laila died? I need to know the date of her death.

"Sure, hang on."

He put the phone down and kept me there in limbo for a few minutes. I'll never understand why the older generation still acts like phones are tethered to the wall.

"Yeah, I have it right here. She died on December 19th, 1801. Why does this matter? Is this significant?"

I wasn't sure how to reply. Or maybe it just took a minute for it to sink in. So many things over the last few weeks conjured up the same reaction from me.

"No kidding," I said, not meaning to include a little chuckle. Sarcasm has always been my go-to response.

"I am not sure why this surprises me, Tom; by now nothing should. She died on my birthday."

I was met with silence from the other end.

"Makes sense." He finally said.

I pulled my phone away from my ear long enough to look at the date. In the weeks leading up to that day, all of my days seemed to blend into one another. I stopped keeping track. The date was the 17th. And then it hit me. Like a ton of bricks.

"Oh my God, Tom! I think I know where he is!"

"That was my next thought, kiddo. Let me get the

information you will need. I'll email you all that I know about the tomb. And Cate, make sure you do not travel with any of this information. The Egyptian government wouldn't take kindly to an American coming to Tomb rob. And I am afraid that is how it would appear, since most people have never heard of it. It has seemed to slip through the touristy cracks."

I tried to delicately address the next pressing topic, but I have not been blessed with an abundance of tact and ended up just blurting it out.

"Tom, Michael knows. I am not sure how much he knows. But he went through your papers in your desk some years ago, and when I came in today, he was in my apartment going through my things. You and I both know he wouldn't take interest in anything that he didn't see as financially beneficial."

He cut me off before I could finish explaining.

"I know what I am up against with him. Leave it to me. You have enough on your plate, but thank you for the heads-up. I'll take care of it. I'll send you the location of my family home in Giza; you will save time and money by staying there. Keep me informed, and be safe. Call me if you need anything."

At the end of the conversation, I had so much adrenaline coursing through my body that I couldn't consider sleeping. I immediately booked my flight, and I spent the night packing and getting ready to go. At 4:00 am the next morning, I received an email.

Cate,

Attached is the map of the location of the tomb.

I hope you don't mind; I alerted an old family friend of your arrival. Please send me your flight information, and he will be at the airport to pick you up.

He is the caretaker of our property and lives on the first floor. He will be available to take you anywhere you need to go. His name is Osama, and you can trust him. Be safe.

Tom

I honestly do not know what I would have done without that man. He always saw and took care of the things I didn't have the foresight to.

I took the early-bird flight, and at 12:30 pm, I landed for the first time in Cairo.

I had only taken a small carry-on, so I skipped the luggage hassle, and after getting my visa stamp, I made my way out of the airport. There, I saw a small older gentleman, dressed in traditional Egyptian attire, holding up a sign with my name on it.

Osama was a delightful man. Happy and smiling.

He spoke enough English to settle my nerves a bit, and he was thrilled to see me. He missed having Tom in the house on his summer visits. I was the first visitor in twelve years, and he was just as excited to have me as I was to be there. I liked him immediately and saw why Tom had such affection for him.

What I learned from him was that he took care of the six-story home while Tom was away, just like his father had done for Tom's grandfather. He had grown up living there and was well educated. He expressed gratitude for the fact that Tom had made sure his studies had always been paid for as a young man, enabling him to focus on what he loved. He was a private tutor and taught English and history to the Children of Giza. He knew the family secrets and was committed to keeping them. His loyalty seemed unwavering. I agreed; he seemed more than trustworthy.

The drive from the airport was my first look at Egypt. The traffic went beyond anything I had ever seen. Cars and trucks were weaving in and out, as though everyone had somewhere urgent to be. Once off of the highway, we shared the road with camels, horses, and Tuk-tuks.

There was sand in every direction. Buildings and palm trees crowded together in long stretches. The closer we got to the house, the more the view was obstructed. but it was a different world than any I had ever seen. The energy was intense.

When we arrived, he got me settled into the fifth floor. After a shower, a quick phone chat with Tom, and a nap, he served me dinner on the rooftop terrace.

I saw, for the first time, how magical Egypt really is.

For when I went up, it was the most magnificent sight I have ever seen. I was face-to-face with the great pyramids of Giza. They couldn't have been a mile in front of me. It was a perfect view.

It was early evening; the sun was just starting to set. The sky displayed colors of orange and pink I had never seen before. I stood there, mesmerized. I cannot accurately describe what that felt like. Standing in front of something I had only learned about in a classroom. I will always look back on that day as one of the most monumental days of my life. Something about those pyramids breathes new life into a person. They did for me, so I have to think I can't be the only one.

I had my dinner, and Osama brought me tea the likes of which I had never tasted. As I sat enjoying the sunset, I experienced my first call to prayer. I can honestly say that I have never felt as peaceful as I did that minute. It felt as if I was exactly where I needed to be. Even if I didn't find Alaa, I knew I had an overwhelming connection to that country that would somehow be my solace.

For the first time in my life, it felt like I was home.

Twelve

Osama woke me before the morning light as the call to Fajr echoed through the city. He knocked on my bedroom door and waited for my answer.

"Miss Cate, we must get an early start. The tomb is hours away; I've packed breakfast for you to eat on the way. Put on something warm, and wear comfortable shoes. The last hour is a hike."

I did as I was told. I got up, braided my hair down the back, and threw on some jeans and a sweatshirt. When I was ready, we got into his little truck and drove for just over three hours. We wound through miles of flat desert, sandy hills, and a never-ending stream of mountains. The last hour of the drive was on a single-lane dirt road going up and between them, with no sign of another person, car, or activity.

We passed dozens of canyons. Each one with its own small entrance. Each one opening up to different-sized desolate areas. Some the size of football fields, others the size of a single American backyard. But all surrounded by the same black, green, and pink granite-looking mountains.

When we did finally stop in front of the entrance to one, it was no different than the countless others we had passed. I am not sure how he knew that was the correct one. I checked the maps' location Tom sent me, and it confirmed that I was in the correct spot.

He walked with me through the oval barren valley to the edge of the farthest mountain. As we stood at the bottom, he handed me a small backpack that contained water and pointed up.

"Forgive me. My health will not permit me to escort you from here; I will stay and wait for you. You should have no trouble finding it. Go straight up until you come to level ground. Look for cacti. They will be spaced out, but if you look closely enough, you will see that there is a pattern. It should take a little over an hour. There is a whistle in the backpack. If you find yourself in trouble, use it. It will echo off of the canyon walls, and I will hear it. I will be here when you come down. Take your time."

Unsure and a bit more than nervous, I started the hike.

The first part of the mountain was a challenge. The incline was almost straight up, and I had to zigzag sideways to keep solid footing. Each step was followed by clouds of dust as sand crumbled beneath me. I started to get the hang of it right about the time I reached a plateau.

Not even halfway up the mountain, it flattened out, just as Osama said it would, and it didn't take too long to spot the cactus. They seemed so out of place and were the only vegetation as far as the eye could see. Not having much faith in myself, I pulled out my phone to check maps again, but I had lost signal. I was on my own.

I followed the cacti for much longer than I had anticipated, and then they stopped. There weren't any more of them to follow. They ceased right in front of a large pointed landmass, with a path on either side. It was as if the mountain kept going but parted to allow a person to walk *through* instead of *up*. I wasn't sure which side to take.

The sun was rising, and it was getting hot. I stopped, sat down, pulled the water from my pack, and scanned my surroundings. I had no clear description of what I was actually looking for and still didn't see anything resembling a tomb. I considered the possibility that somehow, I'd made a wrong turn and had gotten lost.

I got up and walked a few feet on either side of the 'V' formation, weighing my options. The left side went up, and the right side went down. I chose the second route.

The one I chose was jagged and narrow, and so I

held onto the land on my left. Under my tight grip, it crumbled, causing me to lose my balance, fall, and slide down. Once I fell, I didn't even fight it. I just allowed myself to propel down the sandy incline until I came to a stop. I wasn't hurt but sat for a moment fighting back tears. I had so much dependent on reaching the tomb; my emotions were all over the place.

After regaining my composure, I stood, brushed myself off, and surveyed my surroundings again.

Ahead, in the distance, was a patch of sky. I walked until it opened up and became a semicircle of flat ground and a sandy cliff. It was the edge of the mountain. It ended; there was nowhere else to go. I'd reached the end.

As I stepped forward, I spotted something moving. The ground seemed to stir. It rose up and then back down. I took a few steps backwards, not sure what I was seeing. And then my attention was drawn to my right, to something in the corner of my eye. I turned to see a white blur.

It was a dog; Mishmish was running toward me! As he let out a few hyper barks, I bent down and scooped him up into my arms. I have never been happier to see anything in my life.

After he'd thoroughly licked my face and neck and stopped squirming, I bent to put him down. Then I saw what I had really come in search of.

On his knees, wearing a beige galabaya, facing the cliffside, was Alaa.

He leaned forward, placing his forehead to the ground in prostration. He all but blended into his surroundings, and I had mistaken *him* for the ground moving. I silently observed him pray for a few minutes. My heart swelled inside of me, making it difficult to breathe.

When he finished, he sat up and turned to look over his shoulder. He saw me.

He stood and stared at me for a moment. Not moving.

My elation started to fade, and suddenly I second-guessed my decision to come at all. We were facing each other, neither of us bridging the distance between us. The waiting seemed to build more fear than anything else, engaging my fight-or-flight mode. I didn't give into it and instead just waited for what seemed like an eternity.

All at once, he started walking in my direction, stopping just in front of me.

"Catherine?"

He said it slowly, as if he didn't believe it was me.

I nodded, but still, I waited.

He put his arms around me, and I buried my face in his chest. He stood holding me against him for a few blissful minutes before bending down to kiss me.

The most beautiful, perfect kiss. I felt so much relief.

He was still here; he hadn't returned.

I laughed with joy through my tears as he moved stray hair from my face. His hand was under my chin, holding me in place, while he stared.

When I could finally speak, all I could say was,

"I thought you were gone—I thought I had lost you."

He looked down at me with just as much relief as I felt.

"I couldn't. I couldn't leave you."

I didn't want to let go; I stood, holding him. My arms around his waist, breathing him in.

"Oh, Alaa, I am so sorry. I have so much to apologize for. Can you forgive me?"

"Shh. It's okay."

He took my hand and led me to the place where he had just been sitting. We sat down, facing one another, on the edge of the precipice. He kept his head down, took both of my hands in his, and placed them in his lap. After a long pause, his voice shaky, he began to speak.

"How did you know where to find me?"

"A friend helped me find the date of Laila's death, and this was the last logical place."

He smiled in a way that looked bittersweet.

"Catherine, you're so clever. I never should have doubted you. I'll take this as confirmation that you believe me now."

He shook his head and looked out in the direction of the space below. We sat mute for a few minutes. The view was magnificent. We were so high up I couldn't see the ground. There was only a narrow gap between the mountain we were sitting on and the one across from us, but I still didn't see anything resembling a tomb.

"Alaa, where is she?"

He turned and tipped his chin up curtly, as if to point in the direction of the empty slice of canyon beside us. I didn't understand until he said,

"They are below us; we are sitting on it. It is built into the side of the mountain. It was the only way she would be left in peace."

He stood and helped me up. He led me along the edge until we came upon a large piece of sandstone that was jutting out into the air.

As we got directly in front of it, I saw that there were many of the same type of stones that stepped down, one in front of the other. Not cut from the mountain, but somehow installed there, winding down the side of the cliff. They disappeared under what looked to be a man-made overhang. I could see the edges of pillars. There were no ropes or railings on the stairs, and it looked absolutely terrifying.

Mishmish was making his way back up the makeshift staircase. It was obvious he was familiar with them as he jumped from step to step until emerging at our feet.

I poured water into my hand and let him lap it up.

As if speaking to himself—melancholily—Alaa said,

"It is no longer safe to walk down; years of neglect."

He was squatting, one knee on the ground, his head covered in a scarf like I had seen on the heads of many men since landing the day before. It fit him somehow. The clothes he was wearing just looked natural. For the first time, he looked comfortable, and it was displayed even in the way he walked— making him different somehow. He looked up at me, shielding his eyes from the sun with his hand.

"How did you get here?" he asked.

"I have a man waiting for me at the entrance of the canyon. He can be trusted. I'll explain later."

He stood up, pulled me close, and kissed my temple.

"Come, let's go. This is no place to spend your birthday."

And together, we started making our way back down the mountain.

After we climbed the hill I had previously slid down, instead of going straight, I followed him as he curled around it and proceeded up the other side — the side I'd avoided earlier.

We were making our way over rocky terrain for a few minutes until we reached a dead end. Above us was about an eight-foot ledge. He reached into a crevice close to the ground and pulled out a handmade bamboo ladder. He leaned it against the edge, securing it into two small holes in the earth. After he climbed up, he extended his hand down to me. We left Mishmish there, and when we reached the top, I was more than a little confused.

I found that we were standing in a circular area, no larger than a master bathroom, and surrounded by boulders. I put my hands on my hips and cocked my knee out, watching him. Curious to see what he would do next.

He went to one of the boulders and ran his hand along the edge, from top to bottom, until he seemed to find what he was looking for.

Positioning himself on his heels, almost seated, he used his body as leverage and started to pull. In less than a minute, I heard a click, and the rock started to give and move outwards. It was on some type of swivel or hinge. My mouth was hanging open.

He turned to me with a smile, swept his arm in the direction of the newly opened hole in front of us, and said,

"After you."

My lord, people from that time period were resourceful.

I had to stoop down to enter, and once inside, I stood for a moment, taking it all in.

"Oh my God. Are you kidding me? Wow!"

It was about 30 by 20 feet and just as tall as it was wide. There were cushions on the ground the entire perimeter except for the farthest wall, where a firepit equipped with a cooking grate sat. There was at least a year's worth of wood and coal stacked beside it, and I still wonder how it got there. Just above that was a window-sized hole that let in the perfect amount of light. It also allowed for a breeze in the small space, resulting in it being the perfect temperature.

The ground was packed down and almost shone from years of use. The walls were decorated in tapestries and copper plates of some kind, and although everything was old, dusty, and worn, it was unique and inviting, and I was intrigued.

Alaa set about collecting things and putting them into a backpack.

"I built this over two hundred years ago, and it is

a true testament to how things can withstand the test of time if attention is paid to detail. See these beams?"

He pointed to the ceiling.

It was going to take me a while to get used to him referencing timeframes so far gone, but I looked up. Noticing for the first time the three beams that stretched across and down. All spaced the same distance apart throughout the cave. They were beautiful.

"These are olive trees. I had them stripped and cured, then brought here to support the structure. They have resisted change and climate stress and still look as they did the year we put them in."

I was speechless.

"Of course, other than those and the copper, I had to replace everything a few years back when I got here. But it has everything I need and has always been here when I needed a place to stay."

He zipped up his backpack and asked me to turn on my flashlight while he covered the hole in the wall with a perfect circular chunk of wood. When he was finished, he looked around and then headed to the door. After opening it, he paused and looked at me.

"Listen, Catherine, I know you must have a million and one questions, and I promise, I will answer them all. But right now—here—isn't the day or place. We have plenty of time, okay?"

I nodded my understanding, and he leaned down and kissed me on the forehead. After making our way down the ladder, he stowed it away, and Mishmish rejoined us. The three of us walked together back down the mountain.

As we approached the truck, Osama almost ran to greet us.

"As-salam-u-alaikum, my friend."

He did not hide his excitement and immediately went to Alaa, shaking his hand vigorously and embracing him. Kissing him first on one cheek and then the other and repeating over and over,

"Alhamdulillah! Alhamdulillah!" (Thanks be to God.)

Both men were beaming. I did not need to tell either of them anything. Osama knew who he was, and Alaa knew that he knew.

The men exchanged a few words in Arabic as we made our way to the truck. Osama kept looking sideways at him in awe, and honestly, I couldn't blame him.

Thirteen

Growing up in the American foster system, my world constantly changed. There was never any permanence to anything. Everything always felt temporary. As a result, I adapted in some pretty odd ways.

At some point I stopped relying on emotion and started using more logic. Feelings were fleeting, and not just for me. I learned the people around me couldn't be depended on. Humans are emotional creatures by nature and tend to go with what feels good. The sad part is that what feels good one day doesn't necessarily feel good the next. A hard lesson for a child. I lost my faith in the people around me, and with that came the lack of trust.

In addition to that, I adopted a pretty grim view of religion. I felt that the rules of any organized faith were used to keep its followers in line. With a set of rules, people became more docile somehow. More predictable and alike. A group with a common set of principles based on fear of judgment seems to keep them calculable. More from judging each other than from not wanting to upset God, and if people weren't swayed by others' opinions or criticism, they certainly were by the fear created. Fear of the wrath of whatever invisible entity that supposedly holds our eternal rest, or "ever after," in their hands.

None of that ever felt realistic. It went against logic, and being ruled by guilt or fear didn't make sense to me then, any more than it does now.

If you touch a flame and you get burned, it hurts, and you cry. Physical pain produces tears. But what I never gave thought to was why we cry when we get our feelings hurt or someone dies. When we miss someone we love or lose a pet. If we cry when our body is hurt from pain, that is a human body response. What is it inside of us that causes us to hurt, cry, and have pain in our chest when it is emotional damage instead of physical? If it is not a physiological response, then what is it?

And what makes us fall in love? What is it that makes us randomly choose another person and decide that we can't live without them? What makes that specific person worth loving more than any of the dozens of others we come into contact with on a daily basis? And how come we can meet someone who has all of the qualities that should make them perfect for us, but we feel nothing at all? Is it that our soul feels or recognizes them even if our minds do not?

If this is the case, are our souls saturated with memories and feelings from experiences that we don't consciously remember? Is that what creates fears, phobias, or talents that we cannot explain?

If you accept the idea that it is our soul, then it doesn't bring peace or understanding, but instead, it opens up a whole new realm of possibilities and gives birth to a million more doubts and questions. Maybe that is why I never considered it until I had to.

Loving another person as much as I love Alaa will change you. Even under the most normal of circumstances, and he is anything but normal.

Nothing I could have done would have convinced me the way my circumstances did. I didn't have to imagine a soul; I had undeniable proof that I did, in fact, have one. I slowly understood that it wasn't that I had one, but that I was/am one, and that it continuously evolves. Reborn, again and again, to live different lives in different bodies. And although I understood it, I would come to believe it from a whole new perspective. Accounts from someone who had lived many lives alongside my soul.

But, again, I am getting ahead of myself.

So, I will tell you in the same order that he told me and in as much detail as I can; I'll let you decide for yourself.

***

After Alaa and I returned to Cairo, I didn't want to rush him.

I allowed him to open up and tell me what he wanted to, at his own pace. I purposely avoided asking questions and just spent my time enjoying the fact we were together. Not that I wasn't constantly fighting back the urge; I was. But I decided that I would be patient and wait, knowing that eventually he would tell me. He, too, was trying to figure out the best way to explain it all, and so I waited.

We spent time in Giza and walked around the old markets. He introduced me to some local cuisine and showed me things that were still around from his life there. We went to touristy places as well, such as the Valley of the Kings, and on one particularly beautiful night, he and I sailed down the Nile. I could tell he was happy to be back in Egypt.

We spent our evenings on the rooftop, talking about my childhood—or his—and our nights were wrapped up in each other's arms. Sometimes lying awake until the sun came up. The sexual chemistry between us made our union effortless, and we enjoyed each other.

For three weeks, we continued that cycle. Going out during the day, making love all night. With no discussion or plans of our return to England. I had one week left on my tourist visa, and as much as I hated to think of it, I knew I was running out of time and would have to join the real world soon.

We spent the day at the Cairo Museum and stopped by a small market on our way back. That particular day, he seemed a bit withdrawn, and somehow, I knew he was ready to tell me.

So, I wasn't surprised when, after dinner, he asked me to join him on the roof.

Osama brought up a pot of tea, and after we shared a cup with him and he'd gone, Alaa began to speak.

We were both seated on cushions on the ground; he was leaning back against the concrete wall.

"Catherine, I have been considering how to tell you all that I know you want to know. I have decided the best way is for me to tell my story from the beginning. I have never told anyone, in any lifetime, what you are about to hear; forgive me if I struggle a bit through some of it."

He said that, sat for a minute staring at the pyramids, and then looked down and fidgeted with a cushion next to him. He began again.

"The first time I decided to use one of the stones, I didn't have a whole lot of information to go on. I had sought out a man who knew their history and how to use them, but it was all very basic information. All he knew, he had learned from his great-grandfather, and when it came to facts, his memory waned. He was very old and left some important things out. He gave me a few simple rules. Take gold or silver with me; anything plastic or man-made wouldn't travel. I am not allowed to change history, especially the outcome of anything historically significant, and I can't bring back anything tangible from the future. He didn't really know anything else. I left without even knowing what the other stone users knew. So, basically, it was trial-and-error."

"It took several attempts."

"After I found the cave, I went there every day and couldn't figure out what I was doing wrong. I went back to the man, who finally told me what he hadn't before."

"You see, there were originally twelve stones. One for each month of the calendar year. The problem was that not only did I not know that once a stone had been used in a particular month, that month could not be repeated, but once he told me, I didn't know exactly which months were still available. I had to go at the beginning of each month for a few months before it finally worked."

He looked frustrated already, so I decided to hold my questions and let him speak.

"It was 1893. I ended up in London in 1893. One

minute I was in the cave; the next I was walking down the street, amongst everyone else, and everything looked so strange and new. Things had advanced so much in that short amount of time. Horses were still used, of course, but there were cars on the road as well. Not a lot of them, but I had never seen anything like it.

At first, I was so overwhelmed I wasn't sure what to do. I knew some English, but didn't know enough. I had gold but wasn't sure how to use it to get what I needed. Mishmish and I just roamed the streets for a couple of days, taking it all in. It was a far cry from Egypt in every way."

"Eventually, I found an honest merchant who took me under his wing long enough to help me get settled. I had enough money to cover anything I might need. I rented a home in an affluent neighborhood and gradually inserted myself into society. The people of England really didn't care who I was or where I'd come from; all they saw was money. It was obvious I had it, and that is all that mattered."

"Once that part was taken care of, I wasn't sure what to do. I just seemed to be existing in a new world, and I had no purpose. I was more confused than ever."

"On one lonely winter night, I decided to take in an opera. The theater has always intrigued me, and

I was feeling particularly melancholy that day. I thought getting out of the house would help."

"I was seated in the lower balcony alone in a box seat. Halfway through the production, a young lady came and took her seat in the same box. She was a beautiful girl with dark skin and green eyes. But what grabbed my attention more than her stunning appearance was the fact she was holding a cat."

"The cat sat in her lap, not making a move or fuss for the rest of the show. I recalled how Laila used to bring Sheba to every play or major event, and she would similarly stroke her with the same absent-minded love and affection the young lady did. Even in the low theater light, their similarities were uncanny."

"When it was over, I followed her from a safe distance and watched her. The way she walked, something about her sway, and the way she reached up and put her hand to her throat—a nervous tick that I had witnessed Laila do so many times in our years together. It just felt so familiar. She got into her carriage and left, but that wasn't the end of it."

"Shortly after that night, I decided that I needed to improve my English skills and entrusted my valet Abraham with the task of finding me a suitable tutor. I had almost forgotten about it until he informed me that after much searching, he had found one."

"I recall that day being busier than normal. I'd started investing and had a small fleet of trade ships, one of which was coming to port that afternoon. So, when I went into my sitting room for the interview, I was really of the mindset that we would have a short introduction and then start my lessons at a later date. But—as fate would have it—the person he had found as my teacher was the girl from the opera, Lysette."

Alaa looked down as he said her name, staring at his lap for a moment. His tone softened, and he had a look on his face that I can only describe as despair. He looked up and off into the distance. His eyes narrowed as if he were seeing something I wasn't. In his mind, she was before him, and he described her to me.

"She was so tiny. Like a kitten or a bird. The common dress and corset of the time made her appear more so. But her feminine appearance hid the passions that lay within her. She wasn't just beautiful but also brilliant and talented. And although a bit coquettish, she had more self-worth than any woman I had ever known. Always acting as if she deserved no less than the best."

"Her mother was an heiress, her father an Egyptian businessman, and Lysette had been raised a debutante. She was educated in France and was fluent in four languages: Arabic, English, French, and Italian."

He paused again and looked at me, smiling.

"Catherine, in every lifetime, there are a few things about you that remain the same. One of those things is that you write. In one way or another, you are a writer."

"She was a playwright. Being a female writer during that day and age was difficult, and she wrote under a nom de plume. Her fictitious male counterpart received much recognition for her work that she wouldn't have received otherwise, and for years she did well. On any given night, one of her plays would be at one of the many theaters in London."

"Until the word got out that the writer of them was, in fact, a woman. After that, she seemed to write for small theaters and traveling acting companies. I met her after her success had ended. I say ended, not to say that she didn't still write; she did, but never again on that grand of a scale."

"We began our relationship the same day we met. She, the teacher, and I, the student. Three days a week she came to my home, and we got along very well. I enjoyed having someone I could speak my native tongue to, although she scolded me when I slipped into speaking it too often. As time progressed, we developed a sincere affection for one another, and at some point, I just knew.

"For over two years Lysette and I spent not just our lesson time together, but we also enjoyed dinners and operas, and on a few occasions spent holidays in Bath."

I had stayed quiet for some time, and even though I knew the answer, I had to ask,

"Did you have an intimate relationship with her?"

"No, not to that point. I was confused, and as crazy as it sounds now, I was trying to protect her virtue. Anyway, one day, she didn't show up for our lesson. She didn't show up for any lessons that week. After she didn't show up for the second week, I became concerned and went in search of her. I went everywhere trying to find her, but she hadn't shared any personal information with me about where she lived, and other than her name, I knew nothing."

"I finally hired a private detective to locate her, and three weeks later, he came to me with her address."

"After receiving the information, I went to her. I wasn't prepared for what I was met with. She lived in a grand house by the river. From outward appearances, it looked as if she was doing well, but when I went in, it was empty. No furniture, no wood for the fireplace, not even any drapes. It was as if the house was vacant."

"I pushed past her maid and looked through every room until I found her. Lysette lay upon her bed, obviously very ill."

"I took her back and installed her into one of my guest rooms. I called the doctor and kept vigil at her bedside for ten days until the fever passed. She regained some strength, but her diagnosis was grim."

"She had tuberculosis, in those days known as consumption. What it was *called* didn't matter; what it *was was* a death sentence."

"I brought in all of the best doctors and specialists, nurses, and herbalists, and at first, it seemed to be working. For a while, she returned to her old self. We spent those weeks at my house, and all walls were down. Secrets seemed stupid and useless at that point. And even though I didn't burden her with my truth, she told me hers."

"You see, her mother passed away when she was eighteen, which sent her father into a tailspin. There was no consoling him, and he turned to drinking and gambling. Eventually squandering all of the family fortune and dying penniless. Which left Lysette to fend for herself."

"After her career took the turn that it did, she had no way to support herself. Even with the money she made from tutoring me, she couldn't cover her expenses. She had lost everything, at some point selling her furnishings and personal belongings. She did the only thing she could and became a courtesan—a paid escort.”

“As she began to get better, the thought of her returning to that life or having another man touch her was unacceptable to me. I couldn’t allow it. I had to have her for my own. After a lot of persuasion, she agreed to stay with me.”

“She and I lived those final years as if every day was our last. I enjoyed spoiling her, and she let me. She allowed me to shower her with all of the love I had not had the time to give Laila.”

“Knowing someone is going to die gives you an opportunity to do everything you can so that you are never sorry about things left undone or unsaid. I am grateful for every second I was gifted to be with her.”

He paused again, but this time it was to wipe the tears from his eyes before finishing. His next words were more somber and pained.

“There is no agony like watching someone you love slowly die. I watched a beautiful, young, vibrant woman turn into a frail, pale shadow of the person she once was. Knowing that any day she would take her last breath and there was nothing I could do about it.”

“That day came on a Sunday, a few weeks before her twenty-seventh birthday. And, no matter how much I thought I was prepared for it, I wasn't."

"As soon as she died, the second her last breath left her body, I woke up back in 1801. An ending I would repeat many times, always ending up back in 1801, exactly three days before my wife gave birth. I watched you die twice in four days, and it wouldn't be the last time."

Fourteen

After he finished his story, Alaa was spent. Emotionally and mentally drained. I didn't press him for more information. I took him by the hand and led him downstairs, and we curled up in my bed and slept.

When we woke the next morning, we got the first word of the progression of the corona virus. It had been on the news the last few months, but it seemed to become a real concern overnight.

It was rapidly moving through surrounding countries, and from what we understood, we were on the verge of a worldwide pandemic. We made a choice to book our flight home immediately. But because so many were panicked and doing the same thing, as well as the fact we had to secure passage for Mishmish, the first flight available was four days away. Which turned out to be a good thing, because I had woken up with a stomach bug.

I spent that day vomiting and later came down with a fever. I would need to get better before I would be allowed to fly, and so I stayed in bed while

Osama and Alaa tended to my every need.

While I lay in bed, feeling awful, he kept me company. Reading out loud to me or talking more about things in his current life. I could tell he was no stranger to being someone's caretaker.

By the third day, I was feeling somewhat better, and as we sat in my bed having tea, I asked him to tell me more. I wanted to know more. Honestly, I wanted to know everything. I still had so many questions that monopolized my brain.

My request wasn't immediately granted. Initially, he seemed overcome with anxiety. It was so different from the night he told me about Lysette. Although I already knew where the next life had taken him, I didn't reveal my knowledge on the subject. Again, I gave him the freedom to tell me the way he wanted.

He had been lying beside me, with his arm over my belly and his head on my shoulder. He rolled over onto his back and stared at the ceiling for a while before rolling back over to face me. Propped up on one elbow and staring into my eyes, I could see a very clear look of dread. Not just dread, but he looked as if his mind was weighing whether to tell me at all. And then there was resolve, and he began to speak.

"The first time I traveled, I carried the stones with me. It never occurred to me that I would get propelled back to 1801 and that I would relive that part of my life. But I did. Not having the time to get them when Lysette died; it's a good thing that is the way it worked."

"I suffered through Laila and my son's death again, and then my father's. The second time he gifted them to me, there were four, and I wasted no time."

"I left immediately. Once again, I didn't have a plan, but I knew there must be something I was supposed to learn from the future that would eventually help me save them upon returning. I just wasn't sure what. So, I left with a little more knowledge, but nothing that would have prepared me for what I was about to go through. It is the one life I wish I could erase."

He laid back on his pillow and put his hand on his forehead, shaking his head in a no gesture before taking a deep breath and exhaling with a groan.

"It was 1937, and I landed in a town in Poland called Lublin. It's about a hundred miles outside of Warsaw. I realized pretty quickly that time was going to be a stark difference from the last time."

"The technological advances made were astounding, and although that should have been a positive thing, for that part of the world at that time, it definitely was not."

"There were automobiles, airplanes, telephones, and radios. It was unbelievable. It was much more difficult for me to just ease into a life there. As grateful as I was that I at least spoke something other than Arabic, there weren't many people who spoke English."

"I repeated what I had done previously and found an honest shop owner. A beautiful Jewish widower named Jakob who helped without question and set me up in a room in the back of his business. The law had already deemed it illegal for him to own his jewelry business, and it was closed as far as the world was concerned, but he still continued dealing in trade and made his money in the extensive underground network."

"I spent that year trying to learn the language enough to communicate, while he spent the year avoiding antisemitism. We both tried to stay under the radar."

"At first, I didn't understand what was going on. I couldn't read the papers or understand the logistics of the impending talk of war, so I was completely in the dark about what was truly happening. But I didn't need to; fear doesn't need explanation. Hitler had declared himself Fuhrer in 1934, and everyone was scared, and for good reason."

At that time, food was rationed, but if you had money, you could get enough to survive; money was something I happened to have plenty of. Jakob had a network of people he trusted, and they would meet and trade, exchange information, and help one another. Every night he would go out and meet them in out-of-the-way locations and get supplies."

"He risked his neck for me, and he did it out of kindness, not selfishness. I will never forget that."

"One evening he brought someone back to stay with us. A young girl of seventeen."

"Her name was Eve, and she worked for the Lublin Courier, the local paper. She had gotten herself in a bit of trouble when she started writing and distributing fliers against political propaganda. She had intentionally put herself directly in harm's way. Her family was in fear for her and felt it would be best if she lay low for a while. So, she came to stay with us."

"Of course, at that time, all of the anti-Jewish laws were already being enforced. It started with the yellow star of David to be worn on their sleeve, and within a year it was so much more. It was appalling."

"The three of us stayed in all day, every day. We played cards, or they took turns reading out loud. Many hours were spent working on my Polish vocabulary, and I watched as they observed the holy days of their Jewish faith."

"It was difficult. The world had changed so

much, and I couldn't ask the questions I needed to so that I could get caught up, or I would have to explain where I'd come from. I had to act like things flying in the sky or trucks rolling down the road were not shocking. For me, that was especially hard. I made up a feasible story about how I had come to Poland, and it was accepted and never questioned."

"I grew to love Eve. Not as a romantic interest, but more as a kid sister. I was protective of her. She was bright, beautiful, and brave, and she spent so much of her time with her nose in a book or writing. So full of curiosity and promise."

"Once a week, she left the house on her own to take extra food to her family. Her little sister Olga was five years old, and she worried about her the same way I worried about Eve. It was on one of those trips that she returned with Sheba. That is when any doubt was removed, and I knew it was you."

He stopped, got up, and grabbed a bottle of water on the dresser. After handing me two ibuprofens, he sat in the chair next to my side of the bed. He rested his elbows on his knees, hands clasped out in front of him, looking down as he spoke.

"Eve was naive. She was a German Jew. Her mother was German, her father Jewish, and somehow it made her feel safe. As if being half German would protect her. According to Hitler and the law, if someone had three grandparents of

Jewish descent, that person was considered a Jew and would be treated as such. Of course, she carried her father's last name, so it was a false sense of safety."

"I hated it when she left the house. I worried the whole time she was out of my sight. I couldn't go with her to protect her; I had no papers at all. My dark skin and features alone would have caused suspicion. I felt it would bring more harm than good. And so I did the only thing I could do. I sat back and waited each time for her return, and it was hell."

Alaa looked agitated. He got up and began to pace at the end of my bed while he spoke.

"On September 1, 1939, Germany invaded Poland and started World War two. They broke through the meager Polish defense pretty quickly and took over Warsaw. That's when we knew we were in trouble. We moved into an underground bunker that was just outside the back of Jakob's shop. We had stockpiled enough food to last a few months at the most, if we were careful. But we didn't know how long we would go undiscovered."

"In October, the Nazi authorities started rounding up all Warsaw Jews and moved them into the city center. It would later be known as the Warsaw Ghetto. By 1942 they started going into every city, collecting Jewish citizens and transporting them to Warsaw, and we heard disturbing stories of death camps situated all over Poland."

"When Eve heard that they were in Lublin rounding up families, she went home. She had hopes that her family would be left alone but wanted to bring them to the shelter for safety. We couldn't persuade her otherwise. She wouldn't listen to reason. She was going to go no matter what, and when she walked out that door, I felt immediate regret that I hadn't done more to stop her."

"I paced those floors for two days waiting for her, and she never returned. She never came back. Jakob went out to trade one night and heard that she and her family had been taken to the Warsaw Ghetto. What made it even worse was that the Germans were going through the city methodically, street by street; we knew it was only a matter of time before they got to us."

"Within a couple of weeks, I made a plan."

"Jakob asked around and found someone in the network that could secure safe passage for Eve and her family to England. I immediately set up a time to meet with him so that I could pay their way."

"I got my remaining gold, and late one night I went to meet them, but it was a setup—a trap. And before the night's end, I would be in custody."

Alaa came back to the chair beside me, sat down,

and leaned back. He pulled up his sleeve and ran his fingers over a two-inch scar he had on his arm that looked like a burn.

"The numbers are no longer there, but the scar follows me even in another life. Reminding me."

He looked at me then, and for a few minutes he silently stared. Then he stood and left the room. Returning twenty minutes later with a tray containing a silver teapot and two cups. He poured for us both, handed me mine, and then crawled up beside me in bed again. We drank our tea in silence for a bit. Until he said,

"I don't understand how human beings can be so hateful and cruel to one another."

After a long break, he collected himself and started again.

"Eve had been taken to the ghetto; I was taken to a holding cell in the capitol building. The gold bar that I was captured with had our family crest on it, as well as a mint date. That night would be the beginning of the worst and most unfathomable nightmare."

"I was questioned. Every day, some new official would come to question me—for hours. I didn't understand the German language, which seemed to infuriate them. Each day was worse than the one before."

"When I was captured, I had Mishmish with me. They allowed him to roam free around the building and threw him scraps. Oftentimes, I could hear him yelping in pain. They were cruel to him to get to me. I couldn't do anything about it, and Mish was not about to leave me. My cell was in the basement, with a single window at ground level. He would sit outside my window most days and nights. He did that for months, until one day he didn't."

"I got a visit from a man that I would later know as Heinrich Himmler. He stopped killing people long enough to come interrogate me. They knew who I was and were convinced that I had the stones hidden somewhere. I knew then that they were never going to give up. I felt so much relief that I genuinely didn't have them with me. The thought of those bastards having them terrifies me still."

"Anyway, I was held there for a few months and then sent to Treblinka. Treblinka was a death camp, but *I* was kept alive. Later, I was moved to Auschwitz, where I would spend the next two and a half years."

"Catherine, the atrocities I saw there will never leave my mind. I see it in my dreams; I was face-to-face with evil."

"I questioned the doctor who cared for me about Eve and her family every day. I knew she was alive, for the simple fact that I was still in that timeline."

"About a year before liberation, I got the answer I was waiting for. He didn't know about her mother or father, but she and her sister were brought to the camp."

"Although I was treated horrendously, in an effort to keep me alive, a few days a week they gave me extra food. On those days, I would give most of it to the doctor, who would sneak it out and give it to Eve and Olga. It was the only way I could help them."

"In December 1945, one month before liberation, he brought word that she was to be transported to another facility. As Soviet forces advanced, the Germans made every effort to hide their crimes and began either killing the remaining prisoners or taking them on what was later dubbed 'death marches.' Most people didn't survive those thirty-mile walks to their destinations. They either died from the frigid cold, starvation, or got shot along the way when they couldn't keep up."

"I took solace in the fact that long after she had gone, I was still there; I thought she'd made it."

"The day we were freed, I honestly didn't care if I lived or died. What I had witnessed those years were things I wasn't so sure I could live with. But at least I knew that she had made it."

"Before I could even get used to freedom, only a few hours after being rescued, I woke up again in

1801. I knew they had murdered her. She suffered all of those years, only to die at twenty-five, mere hours before she was saved."

"That is what broke me. I never got over it, and it still haunts me. Although I know in my head there was nothing I could have done, I feel tremendous guilt for not being able to protect her. She was so young. She had never fallen in love, had a family, had the chance to pursue her passions or to actually *live*. So much promise and beauty snuffed out for nothing. Because of the Jewish blood in her veins, it disgusts me."

"I returned again to my twenty-one-year-old body, physically healthy but emotionally and mentally destroyed. That time, not only had I not brought back anything to help save my wife and son, but I went back with so much turmoil and unrest that even when they died, I didn't fully feel the weight of it."

"Before my father passed, he again gifted me the stones, and there were three. But I was so damaged, I had no desire to go into the future and see what mankind could offer. It would be many years before I had the courage to go again. I had to heal, and so I waited."

As he said the last words, he stretched out beside me, returning to the position he had been in at the beginning of his story. His arm draped across my body, head on my shoulder.

I wanted to say something, but I had so many questions that I wasn't sure what to say. I knew Eve had to be Evelena Meyer that was on the paperwork in his shed, but what kept going through my mind at that point was who in the world was Ester? One letter in his drawer was written by Lysette, the other by Ester. If he used the next stone to come here, then where was the other one, and who was the other woman?

After consideration, I realized how selfish those particular questions were, and so I kept them to myself. Choosing instead to tell him how sorry I was for the sorrow that life had caused him. I knew that wasn't enough, but finding the right words was hard. He pulled me close, and I rolled over and buried my head in his chest. Then he said something I will never forget.

"Catherine, I'm tired; I'm so very tired."

It wasn't what he said; it was the way he said it. With that one sentence, I understood exactly how much all of the years had affected him. His soul was tormented, and it was his soul that was truly tired.

That night, I struggled to sleep.

Fifteen

My phone started ringing way too early the next morning. After letting it go to voicemail a few times, I got tired of hearing it and answered. It was Tom.

"Hey Cate, how is everything?"

I turned on the light and looked at the time. It was 5:30 am.

"Fine, Tom, you do realize what time it is here, don't you?"

"Yeah, sorry about that, but you're going to want to hear this. The reason I'm calling is to tell you that my house was broken into last night."

I sat up, instantly wide awake.

"Oh my God, are you okay?"

"I'm fine. Nothing was really taken. I mean, the house was ransacked, and whoever it was didn't find what they were looking for. I called the police, and they came out and filed a report, but with nothing really stolen, I'm not sure what will come of it. The reason I'm telling you is that I think we both know who was behind it."

"Michael."

Is all I could say.

"Yes, I have a suspicion he was looking for information on your whereabouts, as well as info on the cave. I had already cleared the house of any paperwork and relocated the journal to a safe place. The only thing that was left out was the page on Laila and the tomb. That is actually the only thing missing. When are you coming back?"

I sat for a minute, trying to make sense of why Michael would want information about Laila.

"We have a flight out today at noon. I'll call you this evening when we are back home."

Tom hesitated before he responded.

"There's something else. The other day at work, Michael asked where you were. When I said I didn't know, he hinted that he had only asked to test my loyalty and that he always knew where you were. So, my next question is, do you think he would have a locator on your phone? And if so, did you use your phone when you went to the tomb? I think he believes that is where the portal is, and honestly, I am concerned for your safety."

My mind went to the day Michael had come to my apartment. He said something that bothered me. He asked me how my trip was, when I hadn't mentioned taking a trip. If he knew I was in Scotland, then had he been there as well?

"I am not sure how to check my phone; I'll be sure and have Alaa do that for me. But either way, we will be back in the UK before the day is out. We can discuss it then. And Tom, thanks for calling."

"Okay, Cate, I'll see you soon."

I hung up and looked over at Alaa. He was awake and staring at me.

"What's happened?"

He asked.

"Nothing to be concerned about just yet. Remember me telling you about Tom? My boss from the paper? His house was broken into last night. I'll tell you all about it later. Right now, I need coffee.

Not the ideal way to start my day.

As we packed and got ready for our return flight, I got more and more angry at the possibility of him tracking me. I felt so violated. I finally broke down, told Alaa what was going on, and had him check my phone.

"Catherine, I am not a technical guy. I wouldn't even know what to look for. But I can see that your location is on, and if someone knew all of your information, they could certainly track you through your location history. When we get back, I want you to ditch this phone, and I'll get you another. That way we can both feel better about it."

I agreed, and a few hours later we were on the flight home.

After landing, it took a while to claim Mishmish, and I was grateful Alaa had left his car at Heathrow in long-term parking. It was late by the time we finally got back to my apartment. I was exhausted and still not feeling well.

It is odd to me the way that certain events in our lives happen and we are immediately different.

I mean, some things come along that force us to forever view our lives completely differently. Somehow separating our time on Earth into two categories. Our life before and our life after whatever event has catastrophically altered it. That is the case for me.

My life was about to take a turn that I never would have fathomed. Even after the unusual circumstances to that point, something else even more shocking would take control of my future, and I never even saw it coming.

***

When we returned, I spent a few days relaxing at home. For weeks I had been running around either with Alaa or trying to find him. My body was tired, and so was my mind. So, I took some time to rest.

He returned to work, left Mishmish with me, and came back to us after each shift.

We spent our time cooking, sitting up late listening to jazz, or playing backgammon. I loved having him there. For the first time in my life, I felt content and happy.

I knew he had more to tell me, but I didn't feel the necessity to rush him. I knew he would talk about it when he was ready. We had all the time in the world. We were just living. Learning and loving each other and enjoying everything that involved.

I was still having periodic waves of nausea and felt increasingly tired. After discussing it with Alaa, I took his advice and made another appointment with my doctor. I mostly stayed around the house waiting for that appointment.

And then one evening we were leaving to go to the market.

It was a day just like any other. I remember laughing at him on the way to the front entrance of my building while Mishmish ran ahead.

It was raining and cold out, and after opening the door, Alaa stepped outside ahead and opened the umbrella. I stepped down onto the sidewalk and looked up. I recall the raindrops coming down in slow motion and the feeling that darkness was closing in around me. The last thing I saw was pink canvas before everything went completely dark—lights out—and that was it—my ending and my new beginning.

Where my old life ended and my new one began. The event that forever separated my life into two parts.

For the rest of my life, my history will always be viewed in two ways.

Before that day and *after that day*.

***

I woke up in the hospital. Alaa at my side, Agnes standing beside him, and Tom leaning against a wall in the corner. I didn't understand at first; it felt like a dream. Tom spoke first.

"Hey kiddo, you gave us a scare!"

My brain was fuzzy; I couldn't think properly. Alaa offered me water, and I sat up and drank a few sips before I spoke.

"How long have I been out?"

Agnes answered,

"Since yesterday, sugar. We have been here all night."

"Alaa, what happened? Why am I here?"

"Catherine, you passed out and have been out for over twenty-four hours."

My head was killing me. I reached around to the back of my neck, where the pain was.

"Take it easy; you've got a nasty bump. You hit the concrete pretty hard."

Initially, I just thought I hadn't been taking care of myself with all of the running around I had been doing lately, and I felt stupid. But after an awkward silence, I looked around the room.

They kept exchanging glances, acting strange. It was only then that I started to get a sick feeling in the pit of my stomach.

Why would Tom and Agnes be there? There was something they weren't telling me, and it was making me more nervous by the minute.

"Alaa, what is going on? You can all remove those fake smiles from your faces; I can see right through you. Just tell me already."

Tom looked across the room at Alaa and nodded to him. It was more for support than permission, and for the first time, I felt fear. I looked back at Alaa.

He scooted his chair forward and took my hand in his. After another long pause, he sighed and, without looking up, began to speak.

"Catherine, you lost consciousness due to your blood pressure being so high."

He stopped and looked up at me. But I knew that couldn't be the whole story, so I waited.

"Look, there isn't an easy way to say this. While you were out, the doctors ran some tests, and this morning, you had a sonogram done to verify what we all suspected. Catherine, your kidneys are shutting down. Both kidneys are covered in cysts, which has caused irreparable damage to both."

I was still staring at him, waiting. I hadn't come out of my fog yet, and I wasn't sure what he was saying. So, I asked,

"What does that mean?"

"You have polycystic kidney disease. It is hereditary, and you have had it for years. Many people go their whole lives without getting diagnosed or even having symptoms until later. Yours is advanced. It would explain the fever, fatigue, and nausea, among all of the other symptoms you have had that I just didn't pick up on."

He stopped again, and his attempt at being tactful was pissing me off. I physically felt awful, and I was already losing my patience.

"Alaa, tell me what else. For Christ's sake, just tell me!"

He responded by saying it all quickly, as if it had been rehearsed, or maybe I was just seeing Dr. Alaa Attia for the first time.

"You need to start dialysis immediately to save

your life and to clean your blood; the toxins are killing you. We will start there, four times a week for now, but it isn't a cure; it is just a treatment. You will need a kidney transplant as soon as possible."

My ears were ringing. I looked at Agnes; the look of pity she had on her face was enough to make me want to scream. In all of the years I had known her, it was the first time I had ever seen that look. I searched for words in my mind, but all I could say was,

"Okay. Then I'll do what I need to do. It will be fine. Babe, I will be fine."

Alaa didn't answer. He looked at Tom and then Agnes, and they understood he was requesting privacy. They both silently walked out of my room.

When they were gone, Alaa adjusted his chair even closer and put his head down onto the hand that he held, and I knew there was more. I braced myself. After a moment, he raised his head and spoke again.

"There's more."

He squeezed my hand, cleared his throat, and told me,

"You're eleven weeks pregnant."

I was struck dumb. How did I not know? Or even suspect?

"What? Are you sure?"

"Positive. Catherine, your kidneys cannot support you right now; they certainly can't withstand the strain of a fetus."

I didn't immediately understand what he was saying, and then I did.

"No."

He looked at me, his eyes pleading.

"Catherine, if you don't terminate, I will lose you both. Please, please reconsider. You don't have to decide right now; you have a few weeks to have it done. But the longer you wait, the longer your kidneys have to struggle for both of you. Do you understand?"

I understood perfectly. My answer was still no. Which surprised even me; I had never wanted children. Or was it that I never gave serious thought to having them? Because at that moment, knowing I was carrying our child, I knew deep down in my soul I would do what I needed to do to have it. In the short time I had known it, I became protective of it, and I was not going to change my mind. He sensed what I wasn't saying.

He sat up and took a deep breath.

"Okay then, first things first. You will get a shunt put in tonight for your treatment and start dialysis first thing in the morning. You'll stay in the hospital until you're out of danger and the toxins in your blood are no longer life-threatening, and you'll go on the transplant list. While I don't in any way agree with your decision, I will support you. We will fight this together."

He kissed my hand, stood up, and opened the door for Tom and Agnes. I could hear him catching them up in the hallway outside.

They both came in after a few minutes and acted as if everything was okay. They were trying to lend me their bravery, and I appreciated that. But I was so exhausted that—at some point—I drifted off to sleep.

I don't remember anything else until early the next morning, when my blood was drawn and my shunt was put in. A few hours later, I was hooked up to a dialysis machine.

It all happened so fast.

It would be something I would get used to pretty quickly. I stayed in the hospital for two weeks, and after I was released, I had to return four times a week. The only plan was to keep me and the child as healthy as possible. It was going to be a long road, but I was far from alone.

***

Gradually, I started to feel better. As the treatment started doing its job, I got stronger. Alaa was so protective, and between him, Agnes, and Tom, I couldn't do anything for myself. They made sure everything was taken care of. Even when I felt like getting out of bed and doing things for myself, they wouldn't let me.

But as the baby grew, so did the strain on my kidneys. I became weak and ill most of the time, and my nephrologist increased my dialysis to six times a week.

We settled into a routine of trips to the hospital and frequent visits to my obstetrician. The people in my life took shifts to take care of my every need. It was exhausting, but I never regretted my decision to keep the baby.

Truth be known, having his child inside of me gave me something to fight for, and after the danger of miscarriage passed, we both threw ourselves into the excitement of it.

Not one time did any of them say anything negative. They were positive, supportive pillars of strength, even on the worst days.

When Alaa and I were alone at night, he lay beside me with his hand on my belly. Both of us were in awe when we felt its strong little kicks; we were in love with our child already.

We spent hours talking about what he or she would look like or whose traits he would have. We went over names and what we dreamed for his future. We shared our ideas and discussed the endless possibilities of what our future held.

I was very sick—there's no arguing that—but I was in love and expecting our first child. As difficult as that time in my life was, I wouldn't trade it for anything.

226

Sixteen

Alaa left on a Sunday for Scotland to collect some things from the cottage before new tenants arrived. He had rented it out for six months to a colleague. He was gone all day, and when he returned, he had the leather folder in his hands and the cardboard tube from the shed under his arm.

I had spent the afternoon with Agnes and was just about to doze on the couch when he came in. Seeing what he was holding, all of the old questions started to run through my mind again.

He dropped the folder onto the coffee table, sat down beside me, and brushed my hair out of my face as he kissed me.

"When were you at the cabin?"

I sat up a little, struggling more than usual with a large belly and my overstuffed sofa. He helped me and then leaned across, using one arm on the back of the couch to hold himself up.

"When I couldn't find you, before I went to Egypt,

I went to the cottage. I got sick and stayed for a few days. When you weren't there, I almost gave up."

He was rubbing a lock of my hair in between his fingers, with a slight smile on his face.

"I saw your letter; it was beautiful and eloquent. You are a good writer—but you always have been."

I smiled back at him.

"Someone broke into the cabin, as well as the shed out back. I am assuming you know what I kept out there. The gold is gone. But there was nothing else to really take."

"What? Oh, Alaa. I am so sorry. It had to be Michael. Did you file a report?"

He laughed.

"Catherine, what would I say to the police? Someone broke into my home and stole three bars of three-hundred-year-old gold that I kept in an old shed out back? Don't you think that might raise some suspicion? No, I didn't report it. I figure he has no reason to break into it a second time, and we don't need the money. I already have enough put away. I'm not going to worry about it, and neither should you."

I rested my hands on my stomach and didn't give any serious consideration to the question I was about to ask.

"Alaa, who is Ester?"

He didn't move from where he was and didn't look upset at the question.

"Are you sure you want to hear the story right now? It's a long one."

He sat up, unzipped the jacket he was still wearing, and headed to the kitchen. After grabbing a bottle of water, he paused and leaned against the doorframe.

"Okay, let me get changed and put on the kettle, and we can talk. I'll be right back."

While he took a shower, I called Tom. After telling him the cottage had been broken into and what was taken, his answer was surprising.

"Cate, I didn't want to tell you with all you have going on, but I guess you should know. Michael left months ago for a short holiday and never returned. He has been missing since February. How long ago was the cottage broken into?"

I thought about it. The last time anyone had been there was when I went at the beginning of December. It was May. He could have been there any time in that five-month span. After I told him that, we both surmised that he had probably made a visit before he left, but it was disturbing news hearing he was missing.

One thing about Michael: his job was the only thing he took seriously. There was no way he would just walk away and disappear from the paper. It left me scratching my head.

After agreeing to meet for supper the following Sunday, we hung up.

When Alaa rejoined me, I told him what I learned. He seemed just as intrigued as I was but chalked it up to Michael's fickle personality. It was probably due to a new girlfriend or interest, and we settled into our late-night discussion.

I was lying on the couch with my legs in his lap as he began to tell the most interesting tale to date.

He didn't look upset or conflicted, which made the story he was about to tell even more unique than the previous ones, and I was excited to hear it.

"Okay, where to begin?" He said, and after a few minutes of drinking his tea and collecting his thoughts, he set his cup down and began.

"Because of the last trip, I waited over seven years before deciding to do it again. I was older than I had ever been in my previous travels at thirty. When I went to repeat the process that time, I had my gold in a bag. Per usual, I was holding Mish, and I guess the trauma from the previous encounter had him scared, because as I placed the stone in the slot, he jumped. He was frightened of a repeat, and I don't blame him. Anyway, I dropped the bag trying to keep control of him, so I left with no money. But that particular time, as luck would have it, it didn't matter."

I interrupted him.

"Tom found that gold and the letter from Lysette in the cave. He wanted me to ask you about it—when the time was right."

It was as if I had snapped Alaa back to the present; he turned to look at me, but more through me, until what I said registered.

"Yes, I should have carried the letter in my pocket. I was more upset about losing that than the gold, to be honest. But I had it memorized and wrote it down later. I'm so glad Tom has the original, though; I have often wondered what happened to it. Thank you for telling me."

As if not to lose his train of thought, he quickly started where he left off.

"The next trip took me to America, 2252. Catherine, you won't believe what happens in the next two hundred years."

He turned to me, positioning his body to face me, and became excited and animated while he talked.

"Everything is different. Humans have realized the damage emissions have on the planet, and so they have gone back to the basics. No cars or jets, and technology has advanced in epic proportions, but there are no clear signs of it. There's no unnecessary use of it. No cell phones or anything else harmful to our brains. Things are simple and uncomplicated. "

"The whole of the population is separated into only two noticeable categories: carnivores and vegetarians. This is done to keep control of the human footprint."

"Scientifically, it just makes sense since people that eat meat emit more gas. It also keeps the animal population down, and there is no animal agriculture. We don't raise and farm animals for consumption. The people that are raised as vegetarians and their families before them have all but lost the ability to digest meat. But that is such a small difference in how things evolve; I am not sure why I started with that."

"We don't use money. Any kind of currency is a thing of the past. Everything we need is either grown, made, or bartered for. There are community fields that we all tend, and there is no hunger. Disease has all but been eradicated, and because we don't use currency, crime is a thing of the past also. We don't even have weapons; there is no need. You would be surprised at how much evil is put to rest once there is no tangible gain. Most crime is born from either lack or greed, and since we have evolved and lack nothing, greed naturally dissipated as well."

"People no longer hold onto religious dogma. It isn't that we don't believe in a higher power; on the contrary, we absolutely know for a fact that God is real, and our faith isn't fear-based or organized. We have a clear understanding of the energy surrounding us every day, and we know we will return to it and be born again from it. It is in all of us. The side effect of that is the death of all religion-based wars and judgments. Everyone coexists beautifully with respect and love and with sincere appreciation for each other and everything we have. The world runs like a finely tuned machine without rulers or restrictions, and we have achieved world peace."

"We have a government, but it is one board of men and women for the entire world. They are not elected and change yearly. It is a lottery-generated selection, and each person has the same chance as the next to be included in it. I believe this is the most monumental thing in all of it."

"The world is divided into three hundred sixty-five equal sections, each section containing an almost identical population. There is one person from each of those sections randomly chosen each year. For the sole purpose of helping mankind. Not to implement laws or rules, but to organize what we need help with. Their main purpose is to help us, and we each take our turn to give back. Every single person will have a rotation in their lifetime, and we all look forward to it with sincere joy and appreciation. It's as if we have genetically evolved to perpetuate peace and gratitude. Anything else goes against our nature."

"He looked so happy while telling me all of the beautiful advances mankind makes, and his smile was infectious. I lay there trying to envision all he was saying. It truly seemed like a dream. He paused for a minute, allowing Mishmish to jump onto the couch beside us."

"There are a few things that took some getting used to. For instance, we are matched up to people that are genetically similar."

"With crops and chores, being paired up makes life so much easier. We are eligible to seek help to be matched with our significant other from the age of eighteen. We have our blood drawn, and it is put into a database. We get a clear list of unmatched people in our region that are genetically compatible, and although there is no legal institution known as marriage, when we are matched and choose to pair up, we do it for life. This is done mainly because conceiving children has become increasingly difficult. The matching system is in place to make reproducing more probable. But, even with that in place, it seems that some couples can and some can't. The couples that *can* usually keep two children and forfeit any born after that to ones that cannot."

"It isn't forced but done out of love and for the good of the whole. To perpetuate human existence. Catherine I can't properly relay to you the genuine love and regard people have for each other. It is a wonder, truly."

"The other thing that took me a while to understand is health care. There are no doctors. I mean, there are people dedicated to each region to help with certain things like accidents or childbirth as needed, but humans have adopted the idea that when it is time to leave this planet, it just is. They don't interfere with natural death. Since disease has become a thing of the past and people eat clean with no pesticides, hormones, or additives, and exercise every day, we either die from old age or, once every great while, an accident."

"Don't get me wrong, we still have things like the common cold, but our immune systems are at a point that they take care of what they are intended to. Basically, doctors are no longer needed, and by allowing our lives to play out naturally, the population is kept at a perfect number for Earth. Like I said before, everything adopted has all been done to ensure the survival of humans and the planet we live on."

"We are completely aware that our future and that of future generations are one hundred percent in our hands. It is our sole responsibility, and everyone takes it very seriously."

"Oh Catherine, living then was so wholesome. I really enjoyed every second. People have morals and integrity, but it's more than that. Neither of those things was based on personal gain or a punishment and reward system. I mean, that is how the idea of God has always been used and perceived. Not just now, but for thousands of years. In the future, it is just part of the human biological make-up not to hurt one another and to do what is right. There is a collective social responsibility, and it is beautiful."

I loved watching him tell that particular story; he was obviously filled with so much joy doing it. But my twenty-first-century cynical side was waiting for the bad part of this tale that surely must come.

Alaa looked at me as if he could see what I was thinking.

"There is so much to tell you, but I must be cautious with some of it."

He stopped short, looked down, and then started again.

"Imagine a world where there are no history books. What I mean to say is that something happened at the turn of the century that wiped out most written word. We are the people that rebuild. Not starting from scratch, but materialistically we restart. All of the literature available had been produced within the fifty years previous, so most of our stories were from older generations who were repeating what their parents, grandparents, and great-grandparents had passed down to them."

"Everyone knew of a past different world, but we had no tangible proof that it ever existed. Our weekends were mostly spent at someone's house or in the gathering area of our street to listen to the older generation tell stories or sing songs. It was our entertainment, and we looked forward to it all week."

"When someone becomes old enough to acquire a home away from their parents, they are either placed in the same neighborhood as their parents, or the housing council finds them one at their request. These areas were set up with complete intention. For example, they all have a postman, but if you are lucky, you would end up in a community with an opera singer or a great storyteller."

"In our sect, before my partner Sarah and I settled there, they didn't have a baker. Sarah was an excellent baker. Each person situated around us had their own specialty. Whether they were a silversmith, seamstress, or carpenter, each had their own talent that added to the success of our particular village. It allowed us to bond and get our needs met. We depended on each other, rather than going outside of our particular group for help."

He lost me after he said "partner." I hadn't heard the name Sarah before, and I guess I was wearing my emotions, because after looking at me, he immediately started explaining.

"I was matched up at thirty-five to my life mate. I had been there by myself for five years, and, to be honest, I was lonely. Sarah was good but very cold and distant, and it didn't take long for me to realize I had been matched incorrectly. I guess I had the expectation of being coupled with another version of you, but that's not the way it happened."

He looked away, suppressing a look of guilt. But I wasn't sure why.

"The housing committee for each area decides where to place each house. We don't pay for housing in the future because it is viewed as a basic human right. Anyway, each couple gets a home. All materials are produced during our time in service. While we spend the year in our *government*, much of our off time is spent planting or harvesting trees for timber or making bricks. Whatever will be needed for others who are in need of a house. We all put into the housing fund in the way of materials, and when the time comes, we all get what we need. All of the members of the community pulled together and helped build the house for the new neighbors, and it was a good system."

"Men, or the dominant spouse, generally build the home right before coupling. Which is what I did. Sarah and I got along fine, but she was not in love with me anymore than I was with her. I tried to give it time, but she was fixated on having a child. That would prove to be impossible, and as the years went on, she became more and more miserable and withdrawn. Each year the failure seemed to be more unbearable for her, and it made our lives difficult. It made me very lonely."

"Ester was our neighbor. She was much older than I and had lost her husband many years earlier in a farming accident. Our bedroom window faced her upstairs office, and I used to sit by the window at night watching her. She had one of those old typewriters that were common in the early 1900s. But for us, they were new again. She sat at that desk and worked for hours under the light of a kerosene lamp."

Alaa smiled, and I could tell he was remembering her fondly.

"I started helping her with her share of the farming, and I did odd jobs around her house when she needed me to. That went on for over twenty years. I knew she was you long before I acted on it. But eventually, even with the age gap, I couldn't deny the pull I had towards her. She was fifteen years my senior. Catherine, you are always so beautiful. You seem to keep the same features, just arranged a little differently, but always beautiful."

He stopped and looked down.

"Anyway, it only happened a few times. Neither of us wanted to hurt Sarah and agreed to shut it down, but our love for each other never waned. She was eighty years old when her body gave out. I was there with her every day for six months. In her final hours, she remembered me. She/you somehow recalled our past lives together."

Again, he stopped and wiped a tear from his cheek.

"When you did pass, it was different than the other times. I was prepared, but I didn't get transported directly back to 1801. I'm not sure why, but I came here first. You died, and then I was here. Only for a few minutes, but Mish and I were on a bus, and Catherine, I saw you."

He looked at me, squeezed my leg with his hand, and repeated himself.

"Babe, *I saw you.*"

Seventeen

The next morning Alaa took me to Dialysis, and while many of my questions were slowly getting answered without having to ask them, I'd gotten to the point that I felt I didn't have to hide my curiosities anymore. We had four hours together, and I couldn't think of a better time to ask some of the pressing ones.

Alaa sat in a chair beside me, scrolling through his phone. Which was unusual for him. Usually when we were together, I had his full attention, but something had him preoccupied.

"What's going on?" I finally asked.

He looked as if he was caught doing something wrong. He looked a little guilty. Like a child with his hand in a cookie jar. He immediately put his phone away and said it was work-related. Something he had been doing periodically the last few weeks. I started the conversation with something I had been needing to say for a while.

"Alaa, I know you paid my debt."

His mind hadn't rejoined me yet; his thoughts were still on whatever it was that had him acting weird. He looked at me.

"Huh?"

I repeated myself.

"I know you paid off my student loans. I've known since Michael came to my apartment. I am sorry I haven't mentioned it till now. Thank you."

He stood up, bent over, and tilted my chin up, kissing me on the mouth and then on the forehead.

"You're welcome; no thanks necessary."

Perfect opportunity to lead into the next question.

"If you knew where I was for three years, why did you wait so long? And how did you find me? Was our meeting on the bus that day an accident or was it planned?"

I now had his complete attention. After scanning the room for anyone within earshot, he scooted his chair closer and answered.

"Okay, here goes. One day I was on the underground going to work when I noticed a newspaper sitting in the vacant chair next to me. I glanced over at it, and it wasn't the article that caught my attention, but a small picture of the journalist who wrote it. Your picture was not that of a stranger. Like I said before, you always keep the same features, just arranged a bit differently. After reading the article, I had my suspicions. The style you have and the way you express yourself are unlike anyone I've experienced before. For me, you are always recognizable, and it can be frustrating. I guess you could say I was being stubborn, because I made up my mind that second that I wouldn't give into it that time. But I couldn't just do nothing either. So, I got the idea that if I contributed to your life in some helpful way, I would somehow be able to avoid everything else."

"Catherine, I had already watched you die seven times. At that point I had loved you and watched you slip away in four different lifetimes, not ever able to change the outcome. I couldn't do it again."

All I could think when he said that was that I was sitting there on dialysis because my kidneys were failing. I was far from healthy, and he was still by my side. How incredibly brave of him.

"Understand, Catherine, all of the other times I traveled, I never had a plan. But the last time, I did. My goal was to learn as much as I could in whatever year I ended up in so that I could carry the knowledge back and save Laila and my son. It was the one thing I knew for sure—that I needed to do whatever I could so that I could save them. I came with the intention of becoming a doctor and focusing on methods of treating patients without medications or special equipment because I knew I couldn't take anything back with me. I intentionally brought the stone, with plans of returning as soon as I felt capable. As soon as I learned enough and had the experience I needed to change their outcome, I was going to use the last one to go back. Whether I was successful or not in that endeavor, I would remove any option of putting myself through another lifetime of attempting to do it again."

"At first, my goals seemed almost out of reach. Simply because I had no identification or school records for a medical school to even consider me. Once again, I discovered that with money, anything is possible. And from the moment I secured them. I was not going to let anything stand in my way."

"Even after I saw that article, I tried to stay away. For almost three years, I refused to even take the 220. But, one day, I found myself intentionally on that exact bus. I think that is why the last time I was allowed those few minutes in this timeline, so that I would know how to find you. It gave me an insight, an insight I wouldn't have had otherwise."

"As fate would have it, after years of avoiding that bus route, the first time I took it, we met."

I pondered his answer for a few minutes. It bothered me in an odd way. Was I standing in the way of his original purpose? Somehow disrupting what should have been? What if I was interfering with the intended outcome—or altering history? It made my brain confused to try and understand. To get my mind sorted, I went on to another question.

"The last time Tom was in the cave, he said a space had been skipped. But the number of travels you have told me about adds up. Did one fall out?"

He actually looked surprised at my question and answered it eagerly.

"That is a good question, and I saw the empty space when I used the portal last to come here. To be perfectly honest, I don't know. But I have my suspicions."

"After considering this for a while, I think that all of the stones showing represent years that have already come to pass. In this life anyway. Assuming that this is my main timeline, I guess that it won't show up here until the year 2252. I think if I had gone to the cave in 2252, the slot certainly would have been filled. It is the only feasible answer I could come up with. Nothing else makes sense."

"Alaa, you know I saw you too. That day, on the bus."

His mind was still on the previous conversation, and it took him a second.

"Wait, you did? You knew it was me?"

"Yes, it was only a few months ago, right before I went to Scotland. I saw you and Mishmish and watched you step off of the bus, but by the time I realized what was happening, it was too late and the bus pulled away. I got off at the next stop and went back to find you, but you were gone."

We both sat not speaking, reviewing the memory of that day. I had one more question, though, and as long as he was answering, I saw no problem in asking.

"What is the paperwork in the cardboard tube, and why do you still carry it?"

He sat back, and his expression changed. I had seen that look before, the whole time he discussed Poland. I hated it and I immediately regretted the question.

"Oh, Catherine. The true evil I saw in humanity during the genocide has never left me. Not a day goes by in any life that I am living that I don't have flashbacks and relive its horror in one way or another. It left so much pain and anger in my heart."

"When I found myself in 2007, I realized that there was a crazy possibility that some of the people involved could still be alive. I made a mental note of each German who had made my life hell. I wanted to make them pay; I wanted them all to suffer the way they had inflicted suffering on so many. Not just for me, but for Eve."

"I needed to find out where she died and how.

Something inside of me needed to know, and I wanted to make sure that she had a proper resting place. I made a list and started investigating each and every one of them. I did that for the first five years I was here."

"But what I realized is that it started to change me. Strange things happen to a person who feeds the hate and anger inside of them. I became consumed with vengeance, and with each disappointment I became more angry, sad, and miserable. Of course, most of those people were long since dead, and only a few of them had stood trial for their acts. It was appalling, really—how many of them died of natural causes and were never brought to justice. I realized it was a losing battle, and I was destroying myself in the process."

"Eventually, I had to let go. I never found out how she died, and maybe that is for the best. But I did find that her sister Olga, although very old, was alive and well. I was able to go meet with her and gift her and her family a substantial sum of money. After that, and donating to the Holocaust foundation, I achieved a level of closure I could live with."

"I am not sure why I brought the lists back from Scotland. Maybe because they consumed so much of my time, or maybe as a reminder of how blessed I am to have lived through it and to have known her at all."

"As horrendous as it was, it is the reason I now have so much appreciation for all I have and hold dear."

As he finished, so did my dialysis, and shortly after that, we left.

***

We went by a specialty baby shop on the way home, something we started doing quite often in those last weeks.

We decided to stay in my apartment for the time being and look for a larger place after the baby was born. So, on the days I felt up to it, we collected supplies for the new arrival.

One corner of the bedroom was already set up with a crib and changing table, and we'd spent the last few months collecting neutral-colored blankets and clothing, agreeing not to find out the sex of the baby until it was born.

We reached home in the late afternoon.

Making our way down the hall, I saw that there was a lady standing by the door. Not the outside entrance; the apartment door. I didn't recognize her, but as we approached, she did seem familiar. I just couldn't place where I'd seen her.

"Can I help you?" I asked.

"Catherine? Catherine Preston?"

"Yes, that's me."

We stood for a moment staring at each other, the feeling of familiarity growing stronger by the minute. And then I realized why; she looked just like me. Almost identical. I asked her again.

"Can I help you?"

Alaa opened the door and said,

"Catherine."

He directed me inside, and—as if he knew the woman—he invited her in as well. But she didn't follow. She stood firm, lingering on the threshold. Alaa spoke to her.

"You must be Cynthia, correct?"

She nodded but never took her eyes off of me.

I looked at Alaa, expecting some clarification on who she was, but I think deep down inside I knew. He didn't acknowledge my look but instead ushered her into the house.

She appeared to be a few years younger, with the same features as my own, with shorter hair, and her frame was just a bit thinner—but basically, I was looking at myself. She seemed embarrassed and shy, but maybe it was just nerves.

Alaa asked us both if we would like tea, and—

even though neither of us answered—he went into the kitchen and put on the kettle. I was left alone with her, still standing just inside the doorway. After removing my coat, she extended her hand and introduced herself to me.

"I'm sorry, how rude of me. I'm Cindy, your sister."

I was already shaking her hand when she made the last statement, and I froze. I couldn't move and just stood there awkwardly holding her hand.

"Pardon me? My what?"

I heard her the first time; I don't know why I said what I said. She repeated herself just as Alaa came up behind me.

"Catherine, I'll explain, but why don't you ladies have a seat on the couch and I'll get the tea first?"

He promptly came back with the tea. After setting the tray down on the coffee table, he took a seat in the wingback chair next to us. He turned to me, placing his hand on my leg.

"Your sister has come all the way from New York."

I blankly stared at him as he spoke.

"Let me start from the beginning. When you got sick, you were placed on the transplant list like millions of others. But even I know that could take many years. From my experience, the best viable donation of a kidney comes from a living relative. So, I began a search."

"I found Cindy a couple of months ago. Before I go any further, don't get your hopes up. Although she would have been a match, after being tested, it was discovered that she too has the same kidney disease."

Suddenly all of the time he was spending on his phone made sense. Before he could finish, Cindy interrupted him.

"Catherine, I never knew I had any siblings. I grew up as an only child. I didn't even find out I was adopted until a few months ago, when the agency contacted me. I wanted to help, and even though it turned out that I couldn't, I still wanted to meet you. I hope you don't mind. Without that call, I never would have known I was even ill. Mine isn't as advanced as yours, but I am lucky because we caught it early, so treatment will keep me healthy enough while I wait. I still have one kidney functioning at 60 percent, the other at 20. So, at the least, I wanted to come and express my gratitude."

I listened to her, and just hearing her talk and watching her mannerisms was mind-boggling. There was no doubt we were related. She looked and acted so much like me. Before I knew it, I felt tears springing from my eyes.

I reached over and threw my arms around her neck.

We sat on the couch, hugging and crying for a while. This beautiful woman was my sister, my blood relation! I was elated. I had gone my whole life alone, and within a few months, I had Alaa and a sister! My child would have an aunt! I couldn't stop crying. I held her and just wept.

Crying from joy is so different than crying from pain. How is it you can instantly love someone? I felt love for her immediately, and I am assuming it is the love that one can only have for a sibling.

When we finally released each other, we both laughed and wiped our tears. We had a whole lifetime to catch up on.

We sat together until late in the evening. When we were both too tired to talk anymore, she returned to her hotel, but we agreed to meet up the next afternoon to continue our visit. I went to bed on cloud nine. I was exhausted but happy, and I went to sleep thinking of the adventures and possibilities that having a sister would bring.

***

I woke up at 2:00 am. My hands and legs were swollen and throbbing, and I had a splitting headache. Alaa heard me stir and asked if I was okay. After explaining that my head hurt, he brought me a Panadol. I took it but couldn't go back to sleep. The pain in my head just progressively got worse.

It became unbearable. My skull felt like it would burst, as if pressure was building up inside. He turned on the light and held me while I rocked back and forth. He got on his phone to call an ambulance; I was in excruciating pain.

When it got to the point I didn't think I could take it anymore, the strangest thing happened.

I felt a bolt of electricity run from my forehead to the nape of my neck. Darkness closed in around me, seeping in from the corners of my eyes like black ink soaking onto paper or fabric. It started to drip and run over my pupils until I couldn't see.

I saw him, and then I didn't. In a flash, my world went completely dark—I was blind.

I screamed out to him and waved my arms in front of me. I had lost my vision and I was terrified.

I heard him say,

"Catherine. Baby, hold on. It's okay. I've got you. Please, just hold on."

And that is the last thing I remember.

254

Eighteen

I was somewhere in between sleeping and awake. That twilight stage you feel just before coming out of anesthesia or waking up the morning after a night of drinking.

I heard strange sounds and wasn't sure if I was dreaming. The noise got louder. Rhythmic beeping, the whirring of a machine and the faint sound of a television or people having a low conversation. I lay listening for a while before being coherent enough to open my eyes.

There was a woman standing just beside my bed. She smiled when she saw me awake.

"Well, there you are."

She reached over and did something near my head and said,

"You're in the hospital, and you're going to be just fine."

I tried to speak, but my lips were somehow sealed. I couldn't open my mouth, and something was preventing me from swallowing. I realized that

I was intubated, and it was quite uncomfortable. I turned my head as much as I could to scan the room.

Gardenias, *everywhere*. Upon each available flat surface were vases and red plastic Solo cups of white gardenias. I yearned to smell them.

On a couch to my right, Tom was sleeping. The nurse walked to him and touched him on the shoulder.

"She's awake."

He dashed to my side. He looked awful, as if he had been in his clothes for days. He put his hand on my arm.

"Cate, my God, everyone will be so relieved."

Everyone? My mind still wasn't putting thoughts into a collective order. Alaa—where was Alaa?

Tom said he would be right back, then left the room. When he came back, a doctor was accompanying him. After a quick pupil reflex test and a few questions that he knew I couldn't answer, he smiled and said someone would be in to remove the intubation tube directly. He elevated my bed and left.

I lay there, half listening to Tom's nervous chatter. He was going on about how Agnes, Cynthia, and he had been taking shifts and that they would be there soon. But as he was speaking, my eyes shifted to my belly, and I was alarmed. It was flatter than it should be. I slowly reached my hand over to feel it, and it hurt. But there was no doubt; I was no longer pregnant. Tears started streaming down my cheeks.

I didn't need to voice my concern; Tom knew exactly what I was thinking. He leaned over the bed, making direct eye contact and speaking slowly.

"Cate, you delivered a beautiful baby girl. Because she was so early, she spent the first few weeks in the neonatal unit, but she was moved last week, and she is thriving. Your daughter is a fighter. Congratulation's momma, you did it."

The relief I felt was almost too much. I had a daughter; I was a mother. The tears I had shed from panic quickly turned to ones of joy. I had a healthy daughter.

Later, the tube was removed, and I was trying to eat ice chips. My throat was so swollen and raw I couldn't speak yet. Sitting up seemed to be a challenge also; I could only assume it was from the c-section.

But the longer I considered that, the more it made no sense. Tom said the baby had been in the neonatal for a few weeks. How long had I been there, and why was I still in so much pain? And why had I been intubated? But mostly I wondered where Alaa was. My mind was in such a fog, and I was so tired.

The nurse came back into the room.

"How's the pain? You can have something if you need it."

I nodded my head, and she returned a few minutes later. After administering medication through my IV, she left, and I fell asleep.

I didn't know how long I had been there, but for the next few days I was very weak, and I slept almost around the clock. Periodically, I woke to see different people in my room. One day Agnes was there, the next Tom or Cynthia, along with an array of different doctors and nurses coming and going.

Soon, my pain meds were reduced, and I stayed awake for longer periods of time.

Agnes was sitting with me one day, and I finally asked her what had happened to me and—more importantly—where Alaa was.

She was on the edge of my hospital bed, holding my hand while she spoke.

"Sugar, you had an aneurysm, which resulted in a stroke. I am not a doctor, and they will tell you more, but right after giving birth, you had surgery to relieve the pressure on your brain. You have been in a coma for over a month. At first, it was medically induced to allow healing, but it wreaked havoc on your kidneys, and we almost lost you."

It took me a while to process what she had said,

but after understanding, my next thought went to Alaa, and so I asked her again.

"Where's Alaa?"

Agnes paused for a moment, then reached over and elevated the bed so that I was almost sitting up. She carefully pulled my cover aside. I saw a clear bandage placed low, almost to my pubic bone and all of the way across. Which was no surprise, but above that one was another larger gauze bandage. She patted it lightly and looked at me. I didn't understand.

Her hand went to the top of my hospital gown, where she pulled it down just enough so that I could see my chest. But it wasn't what I *saw*; it was what I *didn't see*. My fistula was gone. The port used for my dialysis was not there anymore.

Still confused, I looked at her. She raised her eyebrows and looked over her glasses.

"Cate, seven days ago, you had a kidney transplant. It is doing its job, and you no longer need dialysis."

"But how? I've only been on the list a few months."

I still didn't understand what she was trying to say. She was going to have to spell it out for me. And she did.

"Alaa isn't here because he was your donor. He

gave you one of his, and he is two floors down recovering. He is due to be released tomorrow. Honey, he saved your life."

I was stunned and overcome with love and gratitude.

"He seems like a real special guy to me, one in a million. You did good with that one. Before the transplant, he never left your side. He was either here with you or with the baby. Sugar, I don't think he left the hospital once.

The operation appears to have been a success; your body isn't rejecting it, and all signs point to a normal recovery. You're going to be just fine. That is one lucky little girl to have the both of you as parents."

I was crying, and she leaned in and hugged me.

When she pulled away, her face was wet, and she wiped both our eyes with tissue from my bedside table.

"Get some rest, because I have permission to bring the little one by later. Today, you get to meet your daughter."

***

November 2021

The air was crisp and cool, but the sun was shining.

I sat on Tom's porch with a book in my lap, watching our daughter toddle around chasing Mishmish. Her little chubby fingers pointed to the horses just at the edge of the yard. They were hanging their heads over the fence and watching with great curiosity.

"Look, mama!"

She giggled and fell but was only down briefly before getting back up and pursuing the dog again. Alaa ran over and swooped her up into his arms, and to her delight, he spun her around. They were enamored with one another.

He plopped her down onto the yellow grass and, tired from their game, joined her.

He was lying on his back, staring at the sky, his arms across his chest. She was using him as support to lean on while she played with her shoestring. Her black hair lay in soft curls, framing her face. With green eyes and dimples, she is the most beautiful thing I have ever seen.

We came to Toms to recover from the surgery, but after a few months, he didn't want us to leave any more than we wanted to, and so we just stayed. It has become our home.

Cynthia relocated to Scotland to continue her studies and took up residence in the cottage. Every Sunday, she comes for lunch and dinner, as do Agnes and her family. It has become our own little tradition to spend the whole day together.

On long weekends or holidays, they all come, and we stay up late playing cards or bingo, and at Christmas we all take part in decorating the tree. Birthdays are celebrated together also. These are the best memories of my life.

We are a family, and for the first time, I understand what that really means.

I have long since given up on making sense of why and how everything happened the way it did. The last time I brought up Alaa's past was to ask him the only question I had any interest in hearing the answer to.

If I were to die before him, would he return to 1801? He answered,

"I am not allowed to change history. If I didn't change it when I gave you my kidney, I certainly did by having a child."

Since then, he and I no longer discuss much about our other lives; instead, we choose to focus on the one we are living. I have a piece of him inside of me, giving me life. He was finally able to save me, and it has created a bond between us like no other.

I found my soulmate, and that is enough. I have my fairytale ending, prince included. I don't need to know anything else.

So much has changed in the last few years. We are still in the midst of a global pandemic, but my world has remained solid and consistent. I have everything I need and more than I could have ever dreamed in our self-contained bubble. I was, and am, content in it.

Tom received a call from Egyptian authorities in August. Michael's remains were discovered at the bottom of the canyon, just under the tomb. I knew immediately what happened; he tried to take those crumbling sandstone steps on the side of the cliff. As saddening as it is, it was not a surprise to any of us. In the end, his greed was his undoing.

With Michael's death, Tom inherited the newspaper. And although most of his time is spent running it, it is not something he enjoys or ever wanted. It's just how things worked out.

Sometimes I still struggle with understanding the strange and unusual circumstances of how everything lined up just so, to make my present life exist at all, but I have decided to let it go. I cannot possibly have all of the answers—I know that now.

It was almost lunchtime, and I hadn't seen Tom all day. I hollered out to Alaa.

"Alaa, have you seen Tom? Did he go into the office today?"

He reached down and scooped up Laila, coming toward me, carrying her under his arm. She was squealing, and he was laughing. He stopped and transferred her to his shoulders and continued up the steps with her hands on either side of his face. She looked like a monkey, and I giggled.

"Have you seen Tom?" I asked again.

He put her down, and as she headed into the house with Mishmish following close behind, he playfully swatted her behind. Telling her he would be in in a minute.

He looked down at me—half smiling—and handed me a letter from his pocket.

"I don't think we will be seeing Tom again anytime soon."

He patted me on the shoulder, resting his hand there for a moment before following Laila into the house.

I held the envelope in my hands and read the front. It was addressed to me in Tom's handwriting.

I adjusted the blanket I had over my knees and opened it.

Cate,

If you are reading this, I am already gone and am not sure when or if I will see you again.

This old house was always too big for me. I rattled around in it for years, and it deserves a family. You'll find the deed in my top desk drawer; I had it, and the land transferred into your name. Be happy here, as I could never be.

I have split the stock in the newspaper between you and Agnes; I hope you don't mind. I know between the two of you, you will make the right decision on what to do with it. It was never my passion or my calling.

My attorney's business card is also in the drawer; give him a call, and he will explain everything.

Oh, what a beautiful journey this has been. I owe you both a great deal of gratitude. Thank you.

I couldn't be prouder of you if you were my own daughter. Catherine, write your story.

Love, Tom

I sat holding the letter in my lap, considering all that he wrote. At first, I didn't understand where he would go or why we wouldn't see him again. Tears started stinging my eyes about the same time the revelation hit.

I was sure that there was only one thing he would leave all of us for, and that was the chance to be with Caroline. I smiled at the thought.

Alaa rejoined me on the porch holding Laila.

"Are you okay?"

I reached up and grabbed his hand. I didn't need to ask the question; I saw the answer in his eyes. I knew he had given him the remaining stone.

"I think so. I think I will be just fine. I love you." I told him.

He reached down and kissed me, then paused just in front of my face.

"I love you right back."

And then something caught my attention. An old, familiar sound.

I looked to see if he had heard it too, and he nodded. I heard it again, and it was getting louder. It was a cat. He followed me as I stood and walked to the steps, scanning the yard.

Laila spotted her first, pointing her little index finger and excitedly exclaiming,

"Momma, Kitty*! Kitty!*"

I looked in the direction of her gaze and couldn't believe my eyes. There, on the edge of the tree line—running towards us—was Sheba.

"Yes, baby, it sure is."

I took her from Alaa, kissed her on the cheek, and together we went to welcome Sheba.

It seems as though we had all ***finally* come home.**

Acknowledgments.

As an author who travels, this book was written at a very special place. SHARKS BAY UMBI DIVING RESORT, Sharm El Sheikh, Egypt. The staff became family, and the food and the view were magnificent. A huge thank you to Lee and Kimberly Mcgovern; without you this book wouldn't have been published. To Riyaz Delilkhan. Your help went beyond what was expected of any friend; you have my complete gratitude for your input and knowledge concerning everything from formatting and computer issues to editing the cover. For Rafiq Kiswani, Omar from Aussie, and Capt. Abdelrhman. To my best friends here in Egypt, not only did they lend me their names, but also unwavering support! Hala, Osama, Omar, Abraham, and little Laila, I love you all. And finally, to the person who inspired the book, sometimes things happen that can't be changed, and so, we *write a story.* You made my life beautiful. Thank you for loaning me your courage and ambition at a time when I needed it the most.

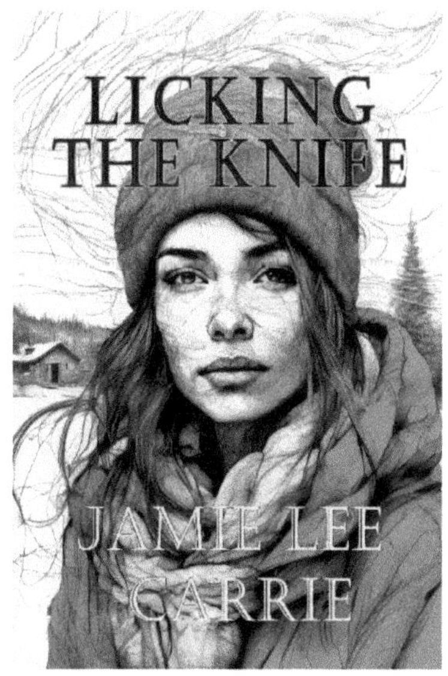

When high-powered attorney Heath Parker finds himself in debt to the Mafia, he plans his wife's kidnapping, hoping her tragic death will clear his slate, while simultaneously making him a very wealthy man.

Leo was not a criminal, but he'd agreed to the task. The fact was, the people Allison Parker's husband owed were the exact same people that Leo's father did. The assignment was the only way to keep his family safe; he had no choice. If he failed, it would mean death for all of them, including his mother and little sister. He wasn't doing it for family honor; he was doing it for their survival. Disposing of a middle-aged, spoiled, and miserable woman would save four lives. And the way he looked at it, he was probably doing her a favor.

But what is supposed to be a quick and cold-hearted transaction changes when a snowstorm entraps them together, captor and hostage, secluded for months from the outside world.

Forced into close quarters, their isolation breeds unexpected and mutual desire and at some point, she becomes worth the risk.

As Leo watches snow fall relentlessly outside the cabin window, he knows *he can't kill her.* But he doesn't know how to save her either. **He doesn't know how to save *any of them.***

272

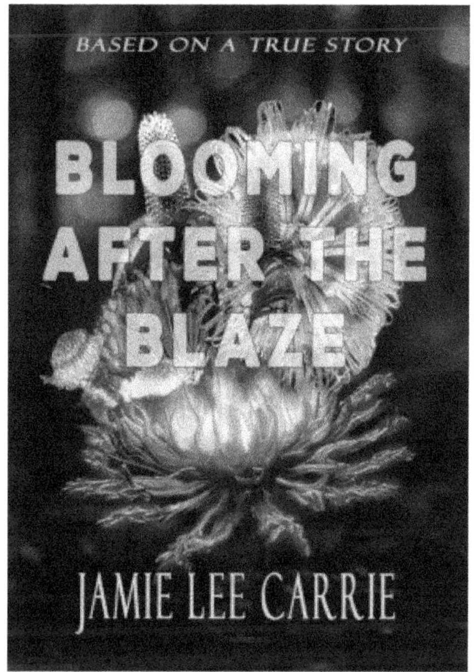

Some seeds only bloom after fire.

In this fiercely personal memoir, Jamie Lee Carrie invites you into a world marked by beauty and brutality, laughter and loss, silence and survival. From the suburbs of Texas to the rooftops of Egypt, she

weaves a story not just of pain—but of persistence. Not just of what was taken—but what still bloomed. Told with unflinching honesty and flashes of unexpected grace, *Blooming After the Blaze* is the true account of a woman who refused to stay broken. It's not a story about running from the past—it's about what you find when you finally stop and face it. It's faith, hard work, and resilience in real time, and it might just make you believe in yourself.

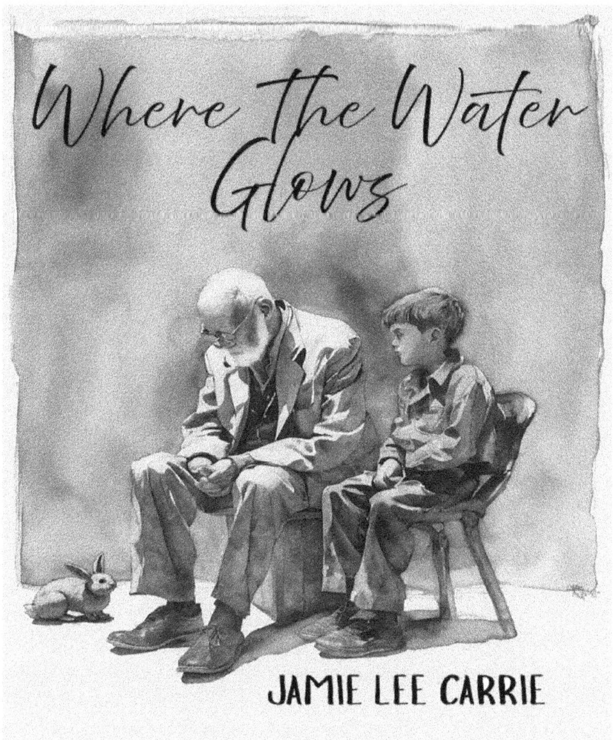

Where the Water Glows is an intriguing novel about the mysterious forces that bind us, the life-altering things we inherit without warning, and what love demands when the stakes are highest. Rich with atmosphere, it invites readers into a haunting and hopeful journey—one where miracles don't come with fanfare, and healing asks more of us than expected. With unforgettable characters and a setting that hums with quiet magic, this is a story that lingers long after the final page.

NEW RELEASE
COMING SOON!
December 2025

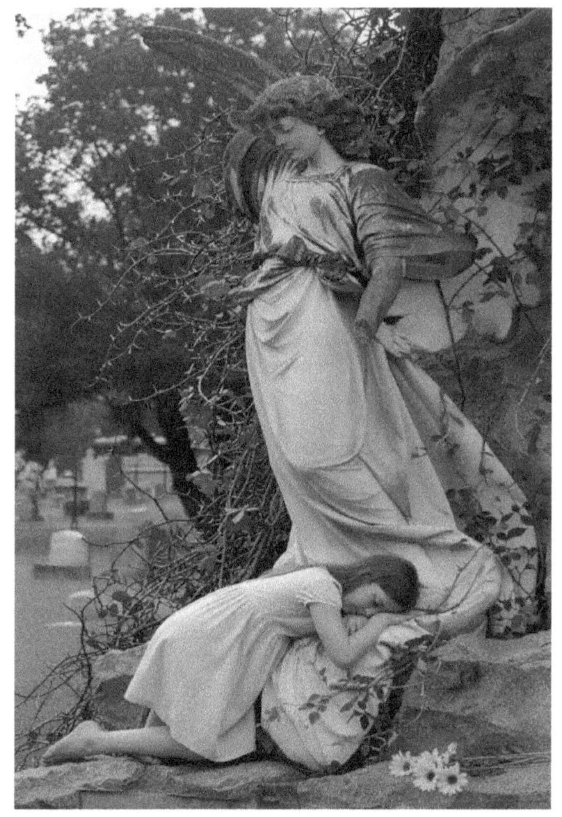

© © *OLIVE'S ONUS*

Book design © Jamie Lee Carrie

QR Code for Author

JAMIE LEE CARRIE

* 9 7 9 8 9 9 9 1 8 6 1 8 2 3 *